PUFFIN BOOKS

BROTHER WULF

WULF'S BANE

Also available by Joseph Delaney

BROTHER WULF
WULF'S BANE

JOSEPH DELANEY

PUFFIN

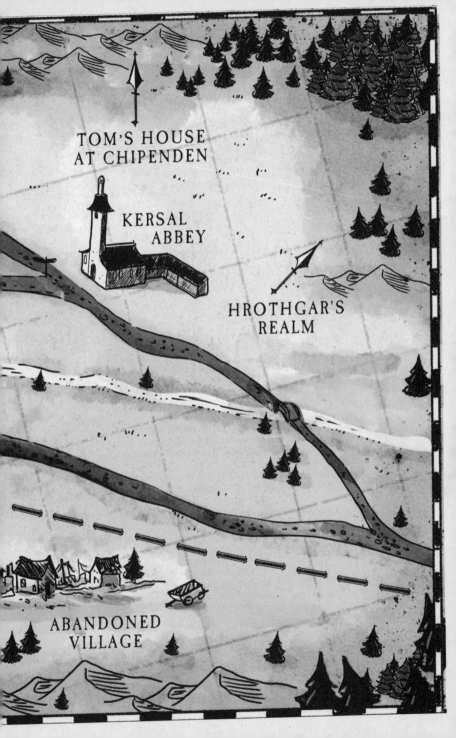

PUFFIN BOOKS

UK | USA | Canada | Ireland | Australia
India | New Zealand | South Africa

Puffin Books is part of the Penguin Random House group of companies
whose addresses can be found at global.penguinrandomhouse.com.

www.penguin.co.uk
www.puffin.co.uk
www.ladybird.co.uk

Penguin
Random House
UK

First published 2021

001

Text copyright © Joseph Delaney, 2021
Map illustration by Alessia Trunfio

The moral right of the author has been asserted

Set in 10/16.5 pt Palatino LT Std
Typeset by Jouve (UK), Milton Keynes
Printed and bound in Italy by Grafica Veneta S.p.A.

The authorized representative in the EEA is Penguin Random House Ireland,
Morrison Chambers, 32 Nassau Street, Dublin D02 YH68

A CIP catalogue record for this book is available from the British Library

ISBN: 978–0–241–41652–5

All correspondence to:
Penguin Books
Penguin Random House Children's
One Embassy Gardens, 8 Viaduct Gardens, London SW11 7BW

MIX
Paper from
responsible sources
FSC® C018179

Penguin Random House is committed to a
sustainable future for our business, our readers
and our planet. This book is made from Forest
Stewardship Council® certified paper.

For Marie

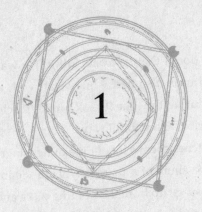

LONG SHARP YELLOW FANGS

Before the sun went down, I would probably be dead.

With less than an hour before sunset, the light was already beginning to fail and I was walking through the mist along a soggy marsh path towards the haunt of the deadly water witches.

I was a spook's apprentice and my master, Will Johnson, was using me as bait. Spooks fight creatures that belong to the dark – ghosts, boggarts and witches just to mention a few – but Spook Johnson was a little different. He called himself a 'witch specialist' and he confined his activities to just dealing with them.

His plan was simple. I would walk about fifty yards in front of him. When a water witch attacked me, he would intervene and kill it.

I had no doubt that he *would* kill it. He was big, strong and fast. Johnson also had a huge staff with a silver-alloy blade. But during the time it took him to reach me, I might die in a horrible and painful way.

Water witches spent a lot of time under stagnant water or buried in the slime of a marsh. When a victim walked by, they would surge up from their hiding place and attack with great speed and ferocity with their sharp talons.

They could drag you down into the marsh or the water, sink their long sharp yellow fangs into your throat and start to drain your blood. At the same time, water or marsh slime would be surging into your lungs and you'd begin to drown.

'Don't worry about drowning!' Johnson had said with a cruel mocking laugh. 'You won't have time to drown, boy. Those witches feed very quickly. You'll die from loss of blood first!'

He thought it was a great joke, but his words terrified me.

My boots were squelching on the slippery ground and there was a thick grey mist which made it impossible to see more than a few feet ahead. Monastery Marsh wasn't that far from the sea but there was a small body of water nearby. I was walking west towards Monk's Hill where there was the ruin of a monastery. But just ahead and to my right was Little Mere, a small lake where the witches were most numerous. This was the most dangerous part of the path and I was moments away from reaching it.

The only thing in my favour is that I did have two weapons that I could use to try and defend myself. One was tucked away in my breeches pocket. It was a small dagger that Alice, the close friend of Tom Ward, had once given to me. Tom was the young spook who worked from Chipenden, and it had belonged to one of his predecessors who'd lived there many years previously. Its blade was also made from a silver alloy – something that was effective against witches and other devilish creatures.

I also had a staff made from rowan wood. Although a witch might flinch at its touch, it wouldn't deter one desperate for blood. Unlike Spook Johnson's staff, mine lacked a silver-alloy blade.

There was a sudden shriek from somewhere to the east, close to the canal. Water witches were most numerous in the marsh and the area surrounding it. But they could also be found along the length of the canal, which ran north from Priestown, through Caster and then all the way up to Kendal. I'd heard such terrifying sounds before and it was definitely the cry of a water witch. At least it was some distance away and in the opposite direction from my line of travel, but witches could sniff your presence from a great distance. Even now one might be heading towards me at speed.

The mist was thickening and the damp was now starting to penetrate my cloak. I shivered partly from cold but mostly from fear.

I began to pray.

My full name was Brother Beowulf because I'd been a noviciate monk before becoming a spook's apprentice. I'd been sent to spy on Spook Johnson and gather information so that he could be tried for heresy and burned at the stake. But Johnson, despite his strength and skills, had been carried off by an unusual and dangerous witch. I'd gone north to ask for help from Tom Ward, the Chipenden spook.

That had led to all sorts of trouble and I'd been in danger of being burned to death myself. Both Spook Johnson and Tom had eventually been imprisoned by the goddess Circe, who would only release them in exchange for Tilda, Alice and Tom's daughter. With my help, Alice had rescued Johnson and Tom but there had been a terrible price to pay.

Now I was called 'Wulf' for short, but despite having lost my faith in God and no longer being a monk, I still prayed to the saints. Mostly they didn't reply. But sometimes I did receive help. It was important to choose the right patron saint.

So, I started praying to Raphael. He was, among other things, the patron saint of safe journeys and, after all, I was on a journey. My destination was Monk's Hill. To get there safely along this dangerous marsh path I badly needed his help.

'Please protect me, Saint Raphael! Please grant me a safe journey and shield me from the Devil's creatures!'

Of course, I didn't say the prayer aloud in case it attracted the attention of a witch. I prayed silently inside my head, which was sometimes just as effective. This particular saint was also supposed to be an archangel, although some monks disputed that. If so, he would be extremely powerful. But perhaps that made it less likely that he'd respond, especially to someone like me. After all, why should such a powerful saint help a boy who'd lost his faith and left his priestly vocation?

The path seemed to be getting even more slippery and I slowed my pace. I was very close to the lake now – it was less than two feet from the path and I could just make out the calm grey surface of the water through the mist.

I thought I heard a noise, the slightest splash no louder than a single raindrop falling into the water, but it was enough to bring me to a sudden halt. I waited there, holding my breath, my heart hammering in my chest. Apart from my own breathing there was silence. I couldn't even hear the distant sound of Spook Johnson's footsteps. For a big man he could be light on his feet. I really did hope he was following me and wasn't lagging too far behind.

I took another tentative step forward, then another. Once again, I was walking along the path but this time more slowly than before.

It happened so quickly that I didn't have time to react. There was a flutter in the mist to my right, a movement over the water, a suggestion of white wings. Then something pushed me really hard, thumping into my right shoulder. It was enough to knock me off balance and I fell to my left, away from the water.

Had the saint pushed me? What had I done to deserve that? Maybe he was unhappy because I had turned away from being a monk?

But then something large surged up out of the water, like a salmon leaping up a waterfall. I had a glimpse of a wet body wrapped in rags. Terrified, I saw tangled green hair, long yellow fangs and taloned fingers reaching towards me. My fall had taken me beyond the clutch of the water witch but the creature landed on two webbed feet close to the edge of the lake and reached down towards me.

I knew exactly what was going to happen to me. The witch was going to grab me and take me down into the depths of the murky water. I would be bled before I could drown.

I was lying on my side but the staff was still in my left hand. I jabbed it towards the witch desperately.

The rowan wood of the staff lived up to its promise – witches were supposed to recoil from its touch. The end of my staff made contact with the left hip of the witch and she took two rapid steps backwards, almost falling back into the water.

I tried to scramble to my feet but I realized that I'd never make it in time. The creature had already recovered her balance and was reaching towards me again, arms outstretched, talons inches from my face, the face a nightmare of fury and ravenous hunger.

But she didn't touch me.

Suddenly she screamed and fell sideways, the blade of Spook Johnson's staff buried in her side. He withdrew the blade and stabbed her again. When his blade entered her body for the third time, she was already dead, lying on her back with one hand trailing in the water.

'What a beauty she is!' Spook Johnson said, his voice full of triumph. 'She's my first kill here – but just the first of many who'll rue the day that I came to this marsh.'

Of course, he was being sarcastic. The water witch was a monster and anything *but* beautiful. I'd read in one of Johnson's books that water witches had degenerated so far that they had lost the power of speech and were no longer human. Her skirt was caked with brown marsh slime and on her upper body she wore a ragged smock which was coated with thick green scum. The webbed feet were terrifying, each toe ending in a sharp talon.

'Did you see that big bird?' Johnson asked. 'It was just above you – seconds before the witch attacked!'

I tore my gaze away from the dead witch. I didn't like telling lies but I forced myself to deceive him. I wouldn't admit that I'd seen anything.

'What bird?' I asked. The last thing I was going to tell him was that I'd prayed to Saint Raphael and he'd saved my life. It might have looked like a bird to Johnson, but birds didn't punch you on the shoulder hard enough to knock you off your feet.

'I wonder if I've just killed Morwena?' Johnson mused. 'She's very old and the queen of the water witches. She likes blood just the same as her ugly sisters but she also has a familiar – a corpse fowl. Maybe that bird I saw was her familiar? Yes, it could well be her! I'll leave the body here as a warning to the rest. Now they'll know what they're up against. Give it a month and there won't be a water witch within twenty miles of here.'

He grinned at me, full of happiness at what he'd achieved. 'Write that up tonight, boy, while it's still fresh in your mind. That should make a great introduction to the latest chapter!'

One of my tasks, in addition to my duties as his apprentice, was to write the story of his life. The working title of the book was 'The Legend of Spook Johnson'. Often, I had to exaggerate what he'd done, but sometimes he more than lived up to the legend that he was trying to create.

You should never underestimate Will Johnson!

It had been a memorable day – the first water witch killed by Spook Johnson since our arrival at the millhouse.

But it wasn't over yet.

That night, just before I drifted off to sleep, I heard a noise under my bed.

It sounded like some small animal was scratching at the floorboards. I could hear it snuffling. It didn't sound like a rat. Maybe it was a hedgehog that had somehow got into the house.

I got out of bed and picked up the candle from the table. It had burned really low but still had a few minutes before it went out. Holding the candle close to my head, I peered under the bed.

I could see nothing. Perhaps there was a hole in the floorboards and the little creature had seen the candlelight and escaped?

I went back to sleep and forgot about it.

Until the next time that it happened . . .

Because that was just the *first* time that I heard scary noises under my bed – the first of many.

THE FATAL GRIP

It was now over two months since that first evening on the marsh, when Spook Johnson had killed his first water witch. Since then, there had been a few close calls. Once, as the light failed, we'd been taken by surprise and surrounded by witches and had been lucky to escape back to the mill. But since then life had settled into a routine and together we'd gradually reduced the threat to almost nothing. Now Johnson only very rarely used me as bait.

He was out patrolling the edges of the marsh and I was alone in the kitchen reading from a slim book about water witches:

A Guide to Water Witches

by

Bill Arkwright

It was a very interesting and useful guide that didn't waste a single word. Arkwright was the spook who'd worked from this house and Tom Ward, the Chipenden spook, had once mentioned him. One short section in this book was particularly chilling.

It was called: *The Fatal Grip*.

The intention of a water witch is to seize and drag her human prey down into deep water where she begins to feed. The witch may attempt to grip a leg, an arm or even the head or an ear but her preferred hold, from which there is no hope of survival, is what may be termed the Fatal Grip.

The witch pushes her thumb into the mouth of her victim and thrusts her first and second fingers, cutting through the skin of the upper throat to meet it. All three of those digits then encircle the jaw. Once achieved, the human victim can never break free. The grip is fatal and death is assured.

I shuddered at the image of that death grip, realizing how close I'd come on several occasions to losing my life.

Just then there was a loud triple-rap at the door of the millhouse and I jumped to my feet nervously.

Who could it be? There were two Quisitors active in the County. Usually they hunted and burned witches but the new Bishop of Blackburn had also directed them to seek out spooks, like Johnson, and bring them to trial.

Once spooks were caught they would be found guilty and burned at the stake too. I was a spook's apprentice. The same could happen to me.

Nervously, I walked through into the large empty front room, opened the door a crack and peered through.

Then I threw it wide open and stood there smiling with relief.

It was Tom Ward, the Spook from Chipenden. He was tall and dark-haired, wearing the cloak and hood typical of our calling. Tom was young for a spook – he didn't look more than nineteen or twenty. He had offered to make me his apprentice but I'd chosen Spook Johnson instead. As I stared at him the smile slipped from his face and I wondered if he was annoyed at me.

'Hi, Wulf! Cat got your tongue? Aren't you going to invite me in?'

'Of course! It's good to see you again!' I stepped aside and waved him into the room. It was basically a store area for the watermill and wasn't used now. So I led Tom through into the kitchen where a steady heat was radiating from the huge stove. It was late November and the winter chill was increasing by the day.

'Is the big man at home?' Tom asked.

My master, Will Johnson, was definitely a big man. He was tall and broad-shouldered, but the biggest thing of all was his belly. It expanded and contracted on a daily basis depending on how many sausages he'd eaten and how many glasses of wine and beer he'd drunk.

'No, he's out on the edge of the marsh hunting for water witches. But he's not had much luck lately. He's already killed a lot of them and the rest have moved north away from the marsh. Now he's starting to get restless and talking about going east to face the Pendle witches,' I said, shaking my head. 'His plan is to kill the Malkin clan witch assassin. He reckons that will flush the rest of them out and he'll be able to deal with them.'

It was a crazy plan. There were several witch clans – too many witches for one spook and his apprentice to deal with.

'Don't worry, Wulf. I'll soon talk him out of it. I've got something else that might interest him. How's he been treating you by the way? He's not been bullying you, has he?'

'He works me hard and can be difficult at times. But I wouldn't call it bullying. He means well. It's just his blunt manner – just the way he is.'

Tom Ward nodded thoughtfully. 'Well, it's up to you. But I'd be glad to take you on as my apprentice, if you ever do change your mind.'

I nodded but didn't meet Tom's eyes. There was a reason why I had chosen to be Spook Johnson's apprentice rather than Tom's, but I didn't even want to think about it.

'This is a great little book,' Tom said, picking it up from the table where it lay next to the piece of paper that I'd been scribbling notes on. 'Bill Arkwright was an expert on water witches and even my own master, John Gregory, accepted his superior knowledge regarding them. I was seconded to Bill for six months so that he could toughen me up. He taught me how to fight with a staff and threw me in the canal – that was his idea of teaching me to swim. Poor Bill's dead now but I'll never forget him . . .'

I nodded and smiled. Tom had already told me a bit about Bill Arkwright on our first journey together when we had gone south to Salford to try and rescue Spook Johnson.

Tom went quiet and neither of us spoke for a while. I was the one to break the silence.

'Sorry!' I said. 'Would you like a hot drink?'

'I thought you'd never ask!' Tom replied with a grin.

So I brewed two mugs of tea and we settled ourselves down at the kitchen table.

'How's Alice?' I asked.

Tom shrugged, but his face immediately became downcast. 'It's nearly three months since Grimalkin took our child and it isn't getting any easier for Alice. It's bad enough for me – and I never even saw Tilda – but Alice is her mother and being without her is a terrible sacrifice. At least it keeps our daughter safe . . .'

The evil goddess called Circe had wanted to drain the blood of their daughter, Tilda, believing that by doing so she would gain immense power. Circe had previously tried and failed to abduct Tilda. But she would try again, and to keep her safe Alice had put her under the protection of Grimalkin, the dead witch assassin who could only visit the earth during the hours of darkness. Tom and Alice had great trust in Grimalkin but I had thought deeply about what it meant and found it very disturbing.

What was it like for Tilda who was now only a few months old? Where was she being kept safe – in the dark? And wouldn't she be terrified and missing her mother? It was bad enough for the two parents but might be much worse for the child.

Circe was still a threat. Alice believed that she was physically unable to leave her underworld, a place somewhere between the dark and the human world. However, she could send demonic entities after us. I too was in danger because I had helped Tom and Alice. Circe had tormented my dreams and intruded into my mind. Alice was a witch, and only a magic feather from the red breast of a robin, given to me by her and always kept in my pocket, was keeping Circe at bay.

Those dreams had been terrible. At first, I'd thought Circe to be a male demon that had appeared on my bedroom ceiling as a terrifying entity without a face, the body made out of sticks. But everything that Circe had done had been part of her deceptions and she had manipulated me as part of her larger plan.

It had been her servant who had snatched Spook Johnson

and then, in the guise of the demon, she'd pretended to help by advising me to go north to bring Tom to Johnson's rescue. Her plan all along had been to eventually lure Alice into her domain and, through her, finally seize her prize – the baby, Tilda – and I'd been her unwitting accomplice.

Alice's magical feather now kept Circe at bay, but it was hard for me to rely on magic. Having been a noviciate monk, despite having lost my faith in God, I still shrank from any contact with dark arts that must surely be tainted by the Devil.

'Any news of the Quisitors?' I asked.

One of them, Father Matthew Ormskirk, had sought to arrest and burn Spook Johnson. That had come to an end when he'd been killed by a boggart. Then his servants had died at the hands of Spook Johnson. But there were still two Quisitors left at large in the County.

Tom took a sip of his hot tea and frowned. 'That's the main reason for my visit. The two of them are very much active,' he said. 'As far as I can be sure, one has stayed in Blackburn and is working from there. The other has come north to Caster. We all need to be on our guard. I think I'm safe enough at the Chipenden house as it's off the beaten track, but I think you and Will Johnson are much more at risk here. It's time that you both moved on because I got a timely warning just yesterday. A farmer I'd once done some work for, and still owed me money, paid off his debt with some important information. He said that someone who lives close to the canal, and is no friend of our trade, had sold vital information to the Caster Quisitor. He'd informed him that a spook was operating from the vicinity of Monastery Marsh.'

That was scary. It meant that the Quisitor knew we were here, and could come hunting for us. It could only be a matter of time.

Tom and Alice were safe enough at home. It wasn't just that they were high above the main roads of the Ribble Valley, on the edge of the fells. Their house was also guarded by a boggart called Kratch who would rip into pieces anybody who tried to enter the garden.

Not only that, Alice could use her magic to call up a mist to befuddle and confuse anybody who tried to find them. I'd already seen it used to great effect.

But Tom was right about us – even before the warning he'd just brought. If the Quisitor thought a spook was operating close to the marsh, we would be easy to find. Then we'd be arrested and after being tortured would be burned at the stake.

I heard the front door opening then – Johnson was back earlier than I'd expected. Now it was my job to make the supper.

Spook Johnson, Tom Ward and I sat at the kitchen table together eating a very early supper. We were tucking into three big plates of tomatoes, bacon, eggs and sausages, all cooked by me. That was one of my most important duties – to keep Johnson's big belly full.

'It looks like you've been doing an excellent job here, Will,' Tom said, swallowing his last mouthful and laying down his knife and fork. 'Wulf tells me that you've cleared the area of water witches.'

'That I have. The job's done. I think my work here is certainly finished – especially after what you've just told me about the Quisitor – and it's time to go. But I've liked working here. The first witch I dealt with was the best kill of all. There was a bird with her – no doubt her familiar. I think I put an end to Morwena, the ancient queen of the water witches!' Johnson boasted.

'Well, it's not impossible that you killed one with a bird familiar – although most just use blood magic – but it couldn't have been Morwena,' Tom said mildly. 'She was killed by Grimalkin years ago. I was an apprentice then, in just my second year, but I saw it with my own eyes. Grimalkin killed her familiar too. It all happened not very far from here on the edge of Monk's Hill.'

Johnson's face betrayed rapid changes of mood. His happiness gave way to disbelief and brief anger but he didn't challenge what Tom had just told him. Then his expression became calm and he just bobbed his head in acceptance before speaking again.

Once that would have caused a big angry outburst, but Spook Johnson had changed and become more tolerant – no doubt because of the shared danger and mutual cooperation we had experienced when surviving the threat from Circe.

'Thanks for the warning about the Quisitor, but we were off anyway. I aim to visit Pendle to do what should have been done a long time ago,' Johnson said. 'I'm going to put an end to those witch clans and make that district safe!'

I thought that Tom would put him straight and point out that it would take an army of spooks to do that, but he didn't argue. Instead, he asked for Spook Johnson's help.

'I was hoping that first you'd do me a big favour, Will. There's a problem near Billinge village, which is about four miles or so south of Wigan, and it would be right up your street. A small clan of witches have taken up residence in the abandoned manor house there. I'd go myself, but Chipenden is keeping me pretty busy at the moment and the list of jobs pending could take a while to finish. And I've another problem – Alice isn't too well at the moment and I don't like to be away from home more than I can avoid. That's why I must turn down your offer of a bed for the night. I need to head back as soon as possible.'

3

NO HOPE AT ALL

We left Johnson guzzling his first bottle of red wine and I walked with Tom as far as the canal. We stood together on the towpath to take our leave of each other. Next to us was the post upon which the bell hung which was used to summon the Spook from the millhouse.

Tom's news had put me on my guard. I glanced along the towpath in both directions, afraid I might see a Quisitor and his men approaching. If it was up to me, I'd leave the mill this minute. But Spook Johnson had little fear of anything and was much more interested in drinking his red wine.

Soon it was going to rain. It was almost dark and clouds were racing in from Morecambe Bay. A few weeks earlier I'd have been wary of the threat from water witches but, after Spook Johnson's endeavours, now I felt perfectly safe. Johnson was full of bluster and he had an ego the size of a city, but I had to admit that he'd certainly got the job done.

Tom was staring at the canal with a sad expression on his face. I remembered our first walk together from Chipenden to Salford just a few months previously, and how he had kept making jokes, despite his sadness at leaving Alice behind at home. Now the present situation seemed to have lowered his spirits.

There was a long pause before he spoke.

'What sort of training is Johnson giving you?' asked Tom.

'Training? Well, he tells me about witches and directs me to read books from the library. I'm still writing the book about him, of course . . .'

'Are you using a notebook to record what you learn?' Tom asked.

I shook my head.

Tom sighed and rummaged in his bag. He pulled out a small book bound with black leather and held it out to me. I accepted it and flicked through the pages, which were blank.

'I thought that might be the case, so I brought this for you. Use it to record things,' Tom advised. 'Even if you have an excellent memory you can't retain everything. Jot down everything you learn from books and when actively on spook's business. Understand?'

I nodded.

'Has he shown you how to use his silver chain? And has he let you practise casting it?' Tom continued.

'No. It stays in his bag. He hasn't used it much since we've been here. He prefers to kill water witches rather than take them prisoner.'

'What about fighting with a staff – is he teaching you that?' I shook my head.

Tom looked annoyed.

I thought back to Tom's offer to train me, and felt a twinge of regret. But then I quickly remembered why I'd had no choice but to turn him down.

'He should be doing those things and more. When I next see him, I'll be having a word about that. Anyway, Alice will be glad to see you, Wulf. I hope it'll cheer her up a bit,' he said.

Johnson had agreed to call in at Chipenden on our way south to Billinge. We were going to stay overnight.

'It'll be good to see her again, Tom,' I told him. 'You said she wasn't too well. I hope she'll soon be better.'

'She won't be better until we get Tilda back and the threat from Circe is finally over. Alice is making herself ill. She's desperately trying to increase the power of her magic. She goes days without speaking a word and she's fasting too. She's lost a lot of weight. All that's bad enough but she's doing it for a reason. She won't talk about it, but I think she plans to confront Circe face to face and fight her to the death.

Alice's magic has always been strong and now she's more powerful than ever. But she's got no hope at all if she pits herself against a goddess. I'm afraid I'll lose them both – Alice and Tilda.'

I struggled to find words of comfort and hope but they didn't come. I didn't know what to say and we both stared at the canal in silence.

I felt the first raindrops on my head and pulled up my hood. Within moments it was pouring down.

'I'll be off, Wulf. See you late tomorrow. Oh! And another thing – I know the boggart knows you by now but it's a bit temperamental at the moment, what with everything being out of kilter. So just to be on the safe side you'd best ring the bell and wait for me before coming up to the house.'

With a wave of farewell, Tom Ward started walking along the towpath south towards Caster. After circling the city to avoid the Quisitor and his men, he'd have to cross the fells to reach Chipenden. He'd be walking all night and well into the following morning.

I turned, left the path and made my way along the stream towards the moat that encircled the mill. Tom told me that it had once been filled regularly with salt to keep the water witches at bay. Johnson didn't bother with that.

'I hope they do attack the millhouse!' he'd once told me. 'I'd kill them faster that way. It would save me the bother of hunting them down.'

Johnson was well into his second bottle of wine already so I left him to it and went up to my room. Working by candlelight, I continued reading Bill Arkwright's book, but this time I jotted down the important facts in my new notebook. You never know when you might need the right information to help you fight the dark.

The following day we were up at the crack of dawn and, after I'd made breakfast, we locked up the old millhouse and set off for Chipenden.

I was carrying Johnson's bag as usual and it was heavy. On top of the usual spook's items, such as small packets of salt and iron and his silver chain, he'd also added several bottles of wine for the journey.

'It's good for walking!' Johnson declared. 'Wine lubricates the leg muscles.'

After skirting Caster, we were soon climbing up into the fells. There was a cool breeze but the sky was clear. Although there wasn't much warmth in the late autumn sun, it was good to feel it on my face. It was a pleasure to be so high with the pastures and woods of the County spread out below us and the sea shimmering to the west. This was a welcome change from the mists and chill dank air of the marsh and, despite the weight of Johnson's bag, I felt glad to be alive.

We walked around the western edge of Parlick Pike, the hill overlooking Chipenden, and descended its southern slope. Soon after we entered the trees, I sensed something in the shadows to our left. It was just the barest hint of movement. I glanced across but saw nothing and thought I must have been mistaken. It couldn't be the Quisitors – they would cause too much noise, riding after us on horseback. Then I remembered how the Malkin witch assassin sometimes followed Tom Ward. Could it be her that was following us? After all, we were a spook and his apprentice – natural enemies. Or perhaps she was following us for a chance to get to Tom through us, and then kill him?

I peered hard into the depths of the forest, but I could see nothing more. It could have been my eyes playing tricks on me. Or Tom's news about the Quisitors had put me on edge. I decided that there was no point in mentioning it to Spook Johnson – he'd only say that I should stop being so jumpy. In my opinion he sometimes recklessly disregarded signs of danger, but he seemed to regard such caution in others as a weakness.

We reached Tom's house just before dark. Following his instructions, I led the way to the crossroads at the withy trees and pulled the rope to ring the bell.

'I never did like that boggart much,' Spook Johnson told me, grumbling at the diversion and delay – I'd explained the situation to him and he'd been muttering about it ever since. 'And it didn't like me either. I always thought it would eventually cause trouble and turn against its master. Old Gregory kept it in line but young Tom was bound to have problems. He lacks the experience to deal with a creature like that.'

I didn't reply but thought Johnson was a fine one to talk. He knew little about boggarts because he only dealt with witches. Ignoring him, I got into a rhythm so that pulling the bell rope became easy. It reminded me of when it was my turn to join the bell ringers at the abbey on a Sunday morning. It was one of the very few things that I'd really enjoyed about being a monk.

At last Tom walked towards us and greeted us both by name, then wasting no time he led us towards the garden. At its edge he paused. 'Kratch! Kratch! Kratch!' he called. 'Keep your distance! Those who walk with me are under my protection and must not be harmed.'

There was a distant growl but nothing more, and after a few seconds Tom walked on into the garden and we followed at his heels. The big lawn had recently been cut and was very trim. I could see that Tom Ward was an expert with a scythe.

'Why's the boggart being difficult?' I asked as we walked across the grass.

'Hard to be sure,' Tom replied, 'but there's something strange brewing. It could be to do with what Alice has been up to. She's been summoning more and more magic and storing it ready for her fight against Circe. Some nights there have been localized thunderstorms directly above the house and garden and the branches have crackled with sparks. Boggarts are sensitive and it's made Kratch a little unreliable. Even though it knows you're protected, I didn't think it was safe to let you cross the garden alone.'

In the kitchen, the table was piled with food. There were steaming dishes of potatoes, carrots, swedes and cauliflower and our large warmed plates were already heaped with thick slices of beef. We sat down and tucked in and it was only when I was full fit to bursting that I mentioned that Alice wasn't seated at the table with us.

'Where's Alice?' I asked.

'She's gone to bed early,' Tom explained. 'I'm getting increasingly worried about her. Gathering so much power is exhausting and, as I said, it's making her ill now. I've tried to persuade her to ease back a bit but she won't listen. All she cares about is destroying Circe and making this place safe for Tilda.'

'Well, Tom, when you're ready to deal with Circe,' Spook Johnson said, pushing his plate away and clasping his swollen belly with both big hands, 'I'll be only too glad to help. You just have to ask.'

'I'll certainly do that, Will,' Tom said, 'and it's good of you to offer. But there's something else I've been meaning to talk to you about. It's young Wulf's training . . .'

I held my breath, afraid of what Tom Ward might say next. Spook Johnson was very sensitive to criticism and quick to anger. But I needn't have worried. Tom had clearly planned what he was going to say with care.

'I know that nobody could prepare Wulf better for dealing with witches and he's learning from the County expert,' Tom continued. 'But I also know that you don't usually deal with other manifestations from the dark, so I wondered if we could remedy that by seconding Wulf to me for a while so that I could broaden his experience?'

Johnson opened his mouth and closed it several times but his face didn't go purple with anger and that was a good sign.

'Of course, it's your decision, Will, because he's your apprentice not mine,' Tom continued, 'but let's say in about a year I could take over his training for about six months? When I was an apprentice John Gregory seconded me to Bill Arkwright to be toughened up and taught about water witches. He also taught me how to fight with a staff and I had lots of bruises to prove it. It was hard, it did me good and I certainly learned lots of very useful things . . .'

'Well, that's settled then,' Johnson conceded. 'A year from now you can have the boy for six months and teach him all about those boggarts and ghosts that occupy so much of your time. But you needn't worry about toughening him up! I'll do that myself. He'll come to you battered and bruised but he'll certainly know how to handle a spook's staff! Now tell me more about the job you have for me? Killing a few witches is exactly what I need!'

'Ha, I can put your mind at ease there,' said Tom, 'because this job is what you're really good at, Will! There are at least three witches working from an abandoned manor house very close to Billinge. They use bone magic and have been raiding nearby churchyards. The danger is that they'll eventually start to abduct living children. Experience tells me that won't happen for a couple of months or so until they've used up the graveyard bones, but the local farmers are worried. I've been summoned to the withy trees by them three times in as many weeks and they're getting tired of my excuses.'

'How far away is it?' asked Spook Johnson.

'Just over a day's walk. I'd have dealt with it myself but things have been pretty busy around here recently, and then I'd rather not leave Alice. I think she's approaching some kind of crisis and I want to be here if she needs me . . .'

Johnson nodded but didn't comment on that. 'Well, Tom, I'll set off there tomorrow before noon. And in the meantime, I'd like to drink a little wine before I go to bed. It helps me to sleep!'

He didn't offer to drink the wine remaining in his bag, so it was a hint that Tom accepted without a blink. He brought two bottles of red wine to the table with a glass and placed them before Johnson. Then we went to bed, leaving Johnson to pour himself a very large glass. I was pretty sure that he'd drink both bottles.

I was given my usual room in Tom's house – the one with the green door where over thirty former spooks' apprentices had slept. They'd written their names on the wall at the foot of the bed.

I was tired so I blew out the candle and climbed into the comfortable bed.

I lay there in the dark slowly drifting off to sleep.

A moment later I was wide awake.

I could hear something scratching and snuffling underneath the bed.

4

PROBABLY NOT SAINTS

My blood ran cold. I was terribly afraid. There had been that same noise under my bed back at the mill. It would happen every two or three nights. On each occasion, when I'd checked under the bed there'd been nothing to see. But eventually I'd told Spook Johnson about it.

'No doubt you're just imagining it, boy!' he'd said, laughing in my face. 'But I look after my apprentices, so just to put your mind at ease I'll go and take a look.'

Johnson had climbed the stairs up to my room, got down on his hands and knees and peered under the bed. Then with a grunt he'd clambered back to his feet.

'Nothing to worry about! No doubt it's just mice. Most likely, there's a whole nest of them running wild under the floorboards. Can't expect anything else living in an old millhouse like this, can you?'

I'd nodded doubtfully and he'd patted my shoulder in reassurance.

But I was not reassured.

And now I was hearing exactly the same noise again but in a different house. It scared me, so I didn't get out of bed and relight the candle. I thought briefly of waking up Alice and telling her about it. But I dismissed the idea. She needed her sleep and had enough problems of her own.

After a while the scratching ceased and I finally managed to get off to sleep.

The following morning Spook Johnson didn't come down for breakfast. After we'd finished eating, Tom suggested a walk.

'I'd like to show you the garden,' he said, 'and there's something I particularly wanted you to see.'

There were three zones to the large garden, and firstly he showed me where the boggarts were held captive. The grass was longer here and each was bound under a large rectangular stone which was positioned flat on the ground.

'This is where I keep the boggarts – there's one bound under that stone and the writing on its surface tells you exactly what type it is and how dangerous the threat that it poses.'

I didn't recognize everything etched into the stone but I could see what appeared to be the Latin numeral for one.

'At the top is the Greek letter *beta*,' Tom explained, 'the symbol that a spook uses for a boggart. See that diagonal line . . . ?'

I nodded.

'That line means it's been bound under that stone. The name underneath tells you who did it. Then at the bottom, towards the right, you can see the Roman numeral for one. It's a warning that bound here is a very dangerous boggart of the first rank. Now I'll show you where we keep the witches . . .'

We walked on underneath the trees until we reached a stretch of grass which had been cleared. There were gravestones set vertically into the ground in the usual manner, but the area before each one was far different to what you'd find in a churchyard. Across the top of each oblong patch dug into the earth, and fastened to a rectangle of stones by bolts, were thirteen thick iron bars. Below that was the dark pit where a witch was imprisoned. I was careful to keep my feet well away from the edge of the nearest one. I could imagine a taloned hand emerging to grab my ankle.

'You can see that we do it differently to Spook Johnson,' Tom said. 'This is the traditional way to bind a witch and keep the County safe.'

'Is this witch alive or dead?' I asked, pointing at the nearest one.

I knew that dead witches could become 'undead' but Johnson had his own method of dealing with them to avoid this, although I'd never witnessed it. He'd once told me that he cut their bodies into pieces and fed them to pigs. He went to such lengths because undead witches were especially dangerous. They could ooze into the ear of a human and possess them, forcing the victim to carry out their will – sometimes even committing violent murders. Water witches only very rarely became undead, which saved Johnson a lot of trouble at the marsh.

'She's alive,' Tom said, gazing beyond the bars, 'and still a real threat. She's been in there for many a long year.'

Back in Salford, Spook Johnson had kept his live witches down in his cellar. They were fed and their cells cleaned out every few days.

'How do they survive in a pit like that?' I asked.

Tom shrugged. 'They use their magic, but slowly get weaker. Of course, they'll eat anything – insects, especially flies. Some of them are capable of attracting swarms of them. No doubt you think this is cruel, and I don't like it either, but it has to be done because some of those witches prey on children and take both blood and bones to satisfy their appetites. Now I'll show you something else – what I really brought you into the garden for . . .'

We walked on until we reached a clearing amongst the trees with a clear view of Parlick Pike and Wolf Fell directly ahead.

'That's my master's grave, Wulf,' Tom told me, sadly pointing ahead.

The grave was a low mound of earth covered with long grass. It was quite close to a wooden bench. I walked forward and read the words on the gravestone:

HERE LIETH

JOHN GREGORY OF CHIPENDEN,
THE GREATEST OF THE COUNTY SPOOKS

'Let's sit down for a while,' Tom said, indicating the bench.

We sat down in silence and gazed towards the fells, listening to the hum of insects and birdsong. It was a quiet calm place. I wondered if Tom was thinking about his dead master. I glanced at him out of the corner of my right eye. He looked really sad again.

'I wanted you to see this. Here was where my master used to teach me,' Tom said at last. 'I would sit down taking notes whilst he'd pace back and forth telling me all about the dark and how to deal with its various manifestations. I loved it here.' He smiled. 'Of course, it rained a lot, being the County. Then I'd get my lessons in the library.'

We sat a while longer in silence. It was peaceful here and I realized what I was missing by choosing to become Johnson's apprentice rather than Tom's.

But despite his friendliness and civilized behaviour, Tom Ward still scared me. The lamia blood of his mother ran through his veins and I'd once witnessed him change into something terrifying when we'd been under attack from the dark. Although roughly human in shape, his body had become covered in scales and his hands had developed sharp murderous talons. Our eyes had met and he'd looked ready to kill me. I'd never been so afraid in my life. I'd wondered if, when so transformed, a madness came upon him and Tom was capable of killing an innocent human without realizing it.

But most of the time Tom was fully human. Lamias were shape-shifters and only a sudden crisis or a desperate need to face a threat and survive induced such a change in Tom. Despite that, my fear of this darkness within him had prevented me from choosing him as my master.

Tom suddenly came to his feet and spoke again. 'John Gregory was a wise and kindly teacher and probably the greatest spook who's ever worked from Chipenden . . .' He paused and swallowed, as if unable to continue speaking. I could see tears glinting in his eyes. 'I must go back to the house now. I have work to do, Wulf. But you stay here a little while longer. No doubt Will Johnson is still snoring in his bed, and anyway Alice has a few things to say to you. She'll be here shortly. She won't keep you long, and after that you could go into the library, find a book that interests you and make a few notes.'

Tom left me and I continued to sit on the bench. I thought about how close he had been to his master and what a terrible thing it must have been to lose him. After a while I heard footsteps approaching from behind and I guessed that it was Alice. There were other noises too – a sudden loud creaking of branches and a constant rustling of leaves, the last ones of the late autumn.

Before I could turn to see what was happening, Alice walked by the bench and stood with her back to the hills staring towards me. I was shocked by two things:

Firstly, the trees on the edges of the clearing, both on her left and right, were very agitated, although there was no wind that could account for their movement. They were flexing rhythmically and bending down towards Alice in an alarming fashion, twigs and withered leaves like snakes striking towards her head but not quite making contact.

Secondly, Alice's appearance had changed for the worse. She looked older. There were lines on her face, which was gaunt with dark circles round her eyes. The sleeveless green dress that she wore revealed her arms to be very thin. Her legs were skinny too where they met her grass-stained pointy shoes. And her hair, which had always appeared dark and glossy, was now dull and greasy.

Alice looked ill.

'It's good to see you, Wulf,' she said, giving me a warm smile. 'I can tell by your face that you're shocked at my appearance, but trust me – I may look a mess but it's not as bad as it seems. Tom worries far too much. It's just that I'm gathering as much power as I can. I'm an earth witch so I draw it from nature, as you can see,' she said, pointing with both hands at the agitated branches left and right.

'Tom's concerned that you're damaging yourself,' I said.

'As I've already told you, it looks worse than it is and it ain't permanent, Wulf. Once I've destroyed Circe and Tilda is safe, I'll relax and go back to the way I was before. But it's you that I've come here to talk about . . .'

She stepped closer to me and bowed forward so that her nose was very close to the top of my head. Then she sniffed loudly three times. I knew she was using magic to learn things about me.

'You're definitely not the seventh son of a seventh son – as I once told you before – and I can confirm that now. But you have the same abilities as one: you can see and talk to the dead and you've got a limited immunity against witches. But there are other things there that I don't understand.'

She sniffed three more times then moved back and gave me another smile.

'There's great power in you, Wulf, but it's something new to me and I don't really understand what it is. You said that you can summon saints to help you?'

I nodded. 'I wouldn't use the word *summon*,' I said, giving a little laugh. 'They don't always come when I call. But when they do, they sometimes really do help me.'

'They're probably not saints,' Alice said, 'but something entirely different. I've seen similar strange things myself. Ain't sure if that's the same as what you've experienced, but I'd really like to help you get to the bottom of it. The problem is, as you can see, that I have other things to deal with first so it'll have to wait for a while. You've still got the feather and the dagger I gave you?' she asked. 'And the mirror?'

I nodded. It was that magical red feather that kept Circe away from me, especially at night when she was at her most dangerous. The dagger had a silver-alloy blade and was a useful weapon against creatures of the dark. The mirror was to contact Alice if I was ever in serious trouble.

'Don't forget to use that mirror if you need to. Got problems of my own, ain't I? But I'd still do my best to help you. Promise that you'll contact me if you need to?'

'Yes, Alice, thanks. I will. I promise.'

'Well, I'll be off. But you stay here and rest for a while. When I left the house, Johnson was still rattling the roof tiles with his snores!' she said with a wicked grin.

'Tom suggested that I go up to the library and study for a while . . .'

'That's a good idea, Wulf. A spook's apprentice needs to keep adding to his knowledge. That's very important. What you know is sometimes the difference between life and death.'

It was only after Alice had left me that I remembered about the scary scratching under my bed. I could have run to catch her up and asked her about it, but I reasoned that she had enough problems of her own.

So I paid a visit to the library instead.

There was one large leather-bound book that caught my eye. I eased it from its place on the top shelf, brought it across to the table and sat down to study it. The book was called *The Spook's Bestiary* and, to my surprise, I noticed that it had been written and illustrated by John Gregory, Tom's master whose grave I had just visited.

It covered the whole range of creatures that spooks had to deal with and there was a big section on boggarts. But the part dedicated to witches had detailed information on the Pendle clans, something that Spook Johnson's books lacked. It seemed that there were more witches in Pendle than I'd realized . . .

The three main clans in Pendle are the Malkins, the Deanes and the Mouldheels. But there are also lesser clans including the Hewitts, Ogdens, Nutters and the Preesalls. Witches often migrate to places that are a source of power and have the right ambience for performing dark magic. It was the brooding presence of Pendle itself that drew the clans to that area.

And Spook Johnson thought he could take on all those witches! Somehow, I had to change his mind about visiting Pendle!

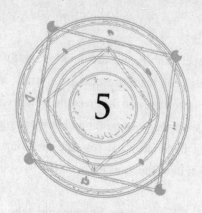

5

THE ABHUMAN

It was very late in the afternoon before Johnson and I set off for Billinge and, having missed breakfast, he wasn't in the best of moods.

There was no sign of Alice but we said a brief farewell to Tom on the edge of the garden.

'It's good of you to sort out that witch problem for me, Will,' Tom said. 'But when you've dealt with that would you mind coming back here first before you go off to sort out the Pendle clans? I've a few thoughts on how it might best be managed. There are a lot of witches in the Pendle district, and although you're the witch expert, my master taught me a lot about the history of the clans and I might just be able to help . . .'

Johnson frowned, opened his mouth as if to make an angry retort, but then I saw him visibly relax. He certainly had changed for the better.

'Aye, I'll do that. It won't do any harm to pool our knowledge and I wouldn't say no to a couple more of those big breakfasts cooked by the boggart!'

With that we went on our way but I wondered what Tom had up his sleeve. My guess was that he was trying to protect Johnson and me from biting off more than we could chew in Pendle. Whatever his plan was it had worked so far. Firstly, he'd distracted Johnson with the spook's business at Billinge and after that was done there would be a further reprieve when we came back to Chipenden.

We made poor progress, Johnson stumbling along bleary-eyed and still not recovered from the previous night's drinking. The two bottles given to him by Tom hadn't been enough – there was also one less bottle of red wine in his bag.

Then, like I did on our journey to Chipenden, I glimpsed something out of the corner of my eye. I was now sure that I wasn't imagining it. I turned quickly and saw something to our rear as it darted out of sight behind a tree. It looked big and bulky and it certainly wasn't a witch.

This time I didn't keep it to myself. 'We're being followed!' I told him.

Spook Johnson spun round and glared at me, almost losing his balance.

'Over there!' I said, pointing back to where I'd seen something.

He growled something under his breath and set off towards the tree that I'd indicated. When we arrived, there was nothing to be seen. Johnson went down on one knee and studied the ground close to the trunk of the tree.

'To be a good tracker like me, you need an eye for detail. And this tells us what's been following us . . .' Using his thumb and forefinger he pulled something from the trunk of the tree, brought it to his nose and sniffed it. Then he showed it to me. It was a few brown hairs. 'A wolf!' he exclaimed.

'But it's daytime,' I protested. 'Wolves hunt at night.'

I should have kept my mouth shut. I could see his face twitching with anger. He hated to be contradicted.

'They're *usually* nocturnal creatures, so this one must be ill or lame and probably driven off by its pack. Well, if it's looking for easy prey, it's made a big mistake! It's no threat to us,' he added with a shrug, and off we set again.

What I'd glimpsed had certainly not been a wolf. I wasn't even certain that there were wolves still remaining in the County. But it was a waste of time pursuing the matter. Spook Johnson could be pig-headed but I'd learned to keep my mouth shut.

We'd barely walked four or five miles when my master called a halt. All that we had for supper was a few small potatoes baked in the fire and Spook Johnson ate most of those.

Now, my belly still rumbling with hunger, I tried to get to sleep whilst he sat cross-legged before the embers of the fire, swigging from his first bottle of wine. At least that meant his bag would be even lighter and easier to carry tomorrow. But then he'd wake up with a terrible hangover again, just like a big bad-tempered bear with a sore head.

He'd probably take it out on me. Although he wasn't really a bully, sometimes he got pretty close to it.

Lying there, I still felt quite uneasy. Who had been following us? I kept listening for the sound of someone approaching our camp. But there was nothing. It took a while, but at last I felt myself drifting off to sleep.

The next thing I knew it was dawn and I was looking up through the branches of the trees into a grey sky. I realized that something had woken me. I'd heard someone speak loudly. But it wasn't Spook Johnson's voice.

Now that voice spoke again.

'Well, little man-thing, I wonder what it'll take to wake up that fat spook?'

The voice was deep but muffled, making each word uttered indistinct. I sat up sharply and craned my neck in the direction of it. Instantly a shiver of warning ran up my spine and I felt very afraid.

It wasn't a man who was looking down at me. The creature was leaning on a huge club, one thicker and far longer than a spook's staff.

'Spook! Spook!' the voice boomed out again. 'On your feet. Let's see what you're made of!'

Spook Johnson sat up and his jaw dropped as he gazed up at the huge creature in astonishment. He lumbered to his feet, rubbing the sleep out of his eyes with the back of his hand.

'Stay well back, boy!' he shouted towards me. 'This is a dangerous abhuman, the spawn of a witch. I'll soon deal with it!'

I'd learned about abhumans from Johnson's books about witches and their offspring. Each abhuman was supposedly the child of a witch and the Devil. That hadn't seemed very likely to me, but one glance at the creature glaring down at me made it easy enough to believe. It was exactly like the description that I'd read. It was big – at the very least a head taller than Spook Johnson, and even wider. But there was no protruding belly, bloated by sausages and wine.

The creature was broad and muscular, and now I realized how Johnson had made his mistake. It was dressed in the skins of wolves which hadn't been properly cured – I was aware of the stink despite the fact that we were several paces apart. It didn't wear shoes either. Its feet were bare, and instead of human toenails it had sharp talons which curved upwards.

It also had a coil of rope across its shoulder. I wondered what that was for.

But in my mind, the thing that confirmed that it was an abhuman was its teeth. Two of them were very large, more like tusks, and they were too big to fit into its mouth. Both protruded over its bottom lip.

Spook Johnson reached down for his staff, lifted it and took a step towards the abhuman.

I had seen Johnson use his staff before, wielding it to devastating effect. Alone, facing seven armed men and using only a rough freshly cut staff, he'd made short work of his enemies. Within less than a minute, all seven had lain dead at his feet, food for the crows. Despite his big belly, Johnson was incredibly strong. He was also fast and skilful with that weapon. I expected him to deal with this abhuman very quickly.

I was wrong.

Johnson attacked in a fury, delivering blow after blow towards the creature's head and body. But each blow was parried by the massive club. Not only was each blow blocked, it was blocked with ease.

And then the abhuman struck back. Two-handed, it whirled the club with incredible force straight at Johnson's head. The spook was fast enough to block the blow but he could only slow its progress. There was a loud crack as Johnson's staff broke into two pieces followed by a dull thud as the club made contact with his skull.

Spook Johnson fell without a sound and I feared that he was dead.

The abhuman turned towards me and spoke, its muffled voice booming through the trees. 'Well, little man-thing, you are coming with me. But first I'll make sure that the fat spook can't follow . . .'

The abhuman walked towards Johnson, then lifted him by his right leg. For a moment I couldn't work out what it intended to do. When I understood I was sickened to the core of my being.

It placed Johnson's leg across its huge knee and there was a crack as the bone snapped. Then the creature dropped the spook onto his back. Johnson's eyes were still closed but he was groaning. Even the pain hadn't managed to wake him. Why had the abhuman done such a cruel thing? Breaking the leg was strangely deliberate, but I wondered why it hadn't killed Johnson outright.

When the creature walked purposefully towards me I scrambled to my feet and tried to run away. I moved fast but the abhuman was faster. Its large heavy hand fell upon my shoulder and gripped it hard.

'Don't try to resist! It will just make things harder for you,' it said, pulling the coil of rope from its shoulder.

I didn't need to be told that twice. My only hope had been to flee, and now I had no chance at all against its incredible strength. The abhuman tied my legs together, then it looped the rope once round my neck and used the other end to bind my wrists. The ropes were tied with surprising gentleness which gave me hope that at some point in the future I might be able to free myself. I still had the short silver-alloy blade that Alice had given me . . .

There was a groan and Spook Johnson staggered to his feet. He immediately fell down again with a loud cry of pain as his broken leg gave way beneath him. But he didn't give up. He seized the nearest half of his broken staff and began to crawl towards us.

The abhuman shook its head. 'What foolishness is this?' it growled. 'I hurt him to stop him following us. This fat spook doesn't know when he's beaten!'

Then the creature lifted me by my legs and flung me over its shoulder so that my head and upper body hung down facing its broad back, the stink of its wolf skins in my face. Then it strode away through the trees.

As we left him behind, Spook Johnson called out to me, 'Be brave, Wulf! Be brave! I'll save you if it's the last thing I do!'

'Save yourself! Save yourself!' I cried, but Johnson didn't respond to that. He just kept repeating his original promise to rescue me, his voice becoming fainter and fainter until distance made it impossible to hear.

His words didn't fill me with confidence. With a broken leg, the best Johnson could hope for was to save himself. He could use his broken staff as crutches, and he needed to drag himself to the nearest farmhouse or to a road where somebody might find him. As for myself, I was puzzled and scared. Why had the abhuman carried me off like this? Perhaps it ate human flesh?

What I'd read about abhumans didn't suggest that they were cannibals, but it was possible. For what other purpose could it have taken me?

After a while, being carried upside down and jostled with each step taken started to make me feel nauseous. I tried hard not to be sick. The creature might react angrily if I vomited down its back.

We travelled through the day until it started to grow dark in the late afternoon. I could hear a faint and rhythmical thudding and twisted my shoulders so that I could see past the creature's waist at what was ahead.

I glimpsed a cottage with a white-haired old woman in the front garden beating a carpet against the low boundary wall.

The abhuman called out, 'Mother Martha! Is it ready?'

Immediately she dragged the carpet indoors and reappeared a few moments later carrying a large hessian sack. The abhuman walked to the wall, reached over and took it from her, holding it in its left hand. No words passed between the two. If she saw me there was no acknowledgement from her. I wondered what was inside the sack.

The abhuman walked on towards two exceptionally tall sycamores and passed between them before suddenly coming to a halt. It lowered me to the floor and now I could see the sky rather than its back and the ground.

My heart lurched with fear. What I saw made me very afraid. The sky was clear but I could see no stars and it glowed a baleful red. I had seen such a sky before when I had travelled into the underworld created by the goddess Circe. The abhuman must be her servant. That was why it had brought me here. I'd helped Alice keep her daughter Tilda from Circe's clutches. Of course, she now wanted revenge.

I could expect nothing but pain and death.

6

SOMETHING REALLY STRANGE

The abhuman began to undo the rope whilst I considered the possibility of escaping.

'There is nowhere to run to now so I will untie your legs, little man-thing,' it growled. 'You would not last long alone here. There are monsters at large that could kill you in seconds. You will be safer inside.'

I wondered what the creature meant by *inside*. And what were the *monsters* that it referred to? We seemed to be in a dense deciduous forest with no sign of any buildings. The only thing I recognized was the two tall sycamore trees behind us.

I was tugged to my feet. Although my legs were now free my wrists were still bound and the rope still circled my neck.

'Walk! That way!' said the abhuman, pointing into the trees.

There was no point in resisting so I obeyed, moving forward in the direction indicated whilst the abhuman followed close on my heels, holding the end of the rope and still carrying the sack in its left hand.

The red glow from the sky increased in intensity, the light reflecting back from the trees and grass giving everything a reddish hue. And then I glimpsed a large building through a gap in the trees. I'd half expected it to be the temple where I had last seen Circe, which was an impressive Greek structure with a portico of marble pillars.

But I was wrong.

As we emerged from the trees, I saw that this was not the dwelling of Circe. Rather than a marble Greek palace fronted by a colonnade, and surrounded by an arid rocky landscape, I was gazing at what had the appearance of a large country house, the grand dwelling of someone from the nobility. It was surrounded by an ornamental moat over which a small bridge arched. Beyond that was a very large sunken lawn, the grass cut very close. Then stone steps led up to the house itself which was very wide, double-fronted with mullioned windows, and two storeys in height.

If this was indeed an underworld as I suspected, it wasn't the domain of Circe. I felt a great sense of relief but then my heart began to beat rapidly again as the abhuman spoke again and fresh fears assailed me.

'Hurry! Hurry! My master wishes to see you!' the creature cried.

Who or what dwelt within that imposing mansion? And how could they know that we'd arrived – unless they used Devil magic?

We crossed the bridge and walked along the raised path that divided the sunken lawn.

'Up! Up!' growled the abhuman as we reached the foot of the steps.

I began to climb and there were a lot of steps – well over a hundred – until at last we faced the closed front door of the mansion and the abhuman tugged the rope to bring me to a halt.

It was then that I noticed something strange about the door. It was wooden and of excellent quality, ornately carved and highly polished. But although it had the usual width it was over twice the expected height, extending upwards as far as the upper-floor windows.

We waited there in silence until that very unusual door opened and someone stepped out to face us. I was the one who broke the silence. I gave an audible gasp of astonishment.

A tall thin giant had emerged.

The giant was probably no thinner than an average human man, but he was almost twice as tall, thus creating that sense of a very narrow body. The creature – for he could not be human, I thought – had to be at least eleven feet tall.

He was dressed like a spook or a monk and wore a long black gown that came down below his knees, and there was a hood pulled forward over his brow which made his face indistinct. He also wore big black leather boots which were extremely large. His hands were big too, perhaps twice the normal span.

The only facial feature I could make out was his nose which was extremely long and slightly hooked like an eagle's beak. The rest of the face, including the eyes, was in shadow.

'I am your loyal and obedient servant, master!' cried the abhuman.

The thin giant took a step towards us. Immediately, the abhuman moved forward quickly, went down on one knee, lowered its head and kissed the left boot of its master. Then it placed the sack on the floor to his left.

'Master!' it cried, holding up the end of the rope. 'I have done your bidding. I have brought you the Spook's apprentice!' Then it kissed his master's boot again.

I was both astonished and puzzled by those words. It seemed that the giant had ordered my kidnapping. What could he want with me?

The giant didn't reply, but with his left hand he reached down and patted the abhuman on the back of its head three times. It was a kindly gesture but it reminded me of the way a human might pet a dog.

Then the giant took the rope, turned and walked towards the open door. Before the rope became taut, I followed.

No sooner had I stepped inside than I saw that the house had been constructed to accommodate the size of its owner. We were in a large unfurnished hallway with a wooden floor, the boards stained black. As he closed the door behind us, I looked up and noted that there were two mullioned windows, one directly above the other. One was the height of my own head; the higher one was positioned for the giant to be able to see out of. From the outside the windows would have suggested two inner floors. But there was only one.

There were also five tall identical doors. The central one was open. The thin giant looked down at me, then he gave the rope a light flick. To my astonishment, it fell away from my wrists even though it had been knotted.

He gestured towards my neck. Then spoke for the first time. 'Remove the rope!'

I had expected his voice to be deep and powerful because of his height, but it was surprisingly quiet and mild. Nevertheless, it was filled with unquestionable authority and I obeyed him immediately.

The rope had gone slack. I pulled it loose easily and allowed it to drop at my feet.

'Now empty your pockets!' he commanded, holding out his huge right hand.

I had items in my breeches pockets that I was very reluctant to surrender. But I was intimidated by his size, and felt unable to refuse him.

I placed the dagger with its silver-alloy blade on his palm, and next the mirror which Alice had given to me. It was a way to reach her and ask for help – help that I now desperately needed. I surrendered my notebook too.

Then, very grudgingly – he saw my hesitation – I placed my magical red feather alongside the other three items. I really needed to keep that. The spell that Alice had placed on it was the only thing preventing Circe from tormenting me after dark.

The thin giant looked carefully at the four items. Then he picked up the feather with the forefinger and thumb of his other hand. He brought it close to his hooked nose and sniffed it. Next, he opened my notebook and flicked through the pages, pausing for a moment to read what was written there.

Then, to my surprise, he handed both the feather and the notebook back to me. 'You may keep these,' he said. 'Put them back into your pocket.' He gestured towards the open door. 'Go inside. You will find everything there that you need and we will talk tomorrow.'

I walked into the room and he closed the door behind me. I heard a key turning in the lock. Alice had once given me a special key that would open any door, but I'd returned it to her.

I was truly a prisoner.

But one glance around the large room told me that this was a very luxurious prison cell indeed. There was a bed, large enough to contain two people in comfort, and enough pillows – each of a different colour – for a dozen sleepers. There were wooden chairs and a comfortable leather armchair as well as two small tables: one was directly under the lower of the two windows and the other was just to its right. Opposite the window table was a writing desk.

Underfoot, the wooden boards were stained black but highly polished. There were three large lambskin rugs, so white they almost dazzled the eye. I imagined the damage that could be inflicted on them by my muddy boots and so I immediately tugged them off, placed them by the door, and walked about in my socks.

I went across to the table under the window. It had a bowl of water, soap and a towel. So I washed my face and hands. As I dried myself, I glanced through the lower window.

The baleful red light illuminated the view from the window. I could see the lawn, the top of the steps, the ornamental moat and, beyond that, the forest.

Then I noticed something really strange.

The sack had gone but the abhuman hadn't moved from the position it was in earlier. It was still down on one knee and its head was close to the ground, its lips kissing the place where the giant's boot had been.

A boot that was no longer there.

7

CALL ME HROTHGAR

Why hadn't the abhuman moved?

Had it been commanded to stay there as some sort of punishment? I thought not, because the giant had seemed pleased with his servant.

I watched for a few moments but there wasn't the slightest hint of stirring. The abhuman was immobile, just like a statue.

Then I glanced towards the other table on my right. On it was a dish covered with a white cloth and beside it was a large glass of water. My captor had promised that the room contained everything that I would need. Well, I hadn't eaten all day and my belly was rumbling . . .

I lifted the cloth and was grateful for what was revealed, although it was just a large piece of crumbly County cheese. I began to eat it wolfishly. I would have preferred a hot meal of potatoes and chicken, lamb or beef. Or perhaps bacon, eggs and tomatoes. But this was more than welcome.

A small portion of cheese was what most spooks traditionally lived on when they were soon to face the dark. It maintained physical strength, yet that limited diet somehow made their job easier. You didn't want to fight boggarts or witches on a full stomach. Of course, Spook Johnson ignored that diet, but I knew that Tom Ward kept to it. Had I been provided with this because the thin giant thought it was what a spook's apprentice ate?

I forced myself to leave half of the cheese and only drank half of the glass of water. I intended to sleep and there was no guarantee of any breakfast when I awoke. I didn't undress but just lay down on top of the bedcover. I was exhausted. Despite my predicament, sleep wasn't long in coming.

When I awoke I felt rested and clear-headed. I climbed off the bed and looked through the lower window. Even though I sensed that several hours had passed, it was still night with the same red sky. In this underworld the sun would never rise.

The abhuman was still in exactly the same kneeling position. How could it do that? Was it bewitched or in some kind of suspended animation waiting there, barely alive, until its master needed it again?

I ate the remainder of the cheese and drained the glass of water. Then I walked to the door and listened carefully at the keyhole. I could hear nothing. All was silent. Perhaps the giant was asleep in one of the other rooms? If so, I might never get another chance as good as this.

I intended to escape.

Firstly, I pulled on my boots and laced them. Then I made my way back to the door, being careful not to step on any of the white lambskin rugs. Then I knelt in front of the door with my forehead almost touching it.

I was going to pray to Saint Quentin, the patron saint of locks and locksmiths. He'd helped me before and I hoped that he would do so again.

I said my prayer aloud but kept my voice very low. 'Saint Quentin, I beseech thee. Please open this door so that I may escape this prison and be free of these servants of the Devil!'

Nothing happened, but you had to be persistent. Saints rarely answered your first prayer.

I repeated the prayer. There was still no response.

The next thing I could try was to beat my head against the door. That usually worked. Inflicting pain on yourself often got a saint's attention. But here I had a problem. Banging my head against the door might make enough noise to awake the thin giant and that was the last thing I wished for. I didn't think he'd be best pleased if he caught me in the act of trying to escape. I felt certain that I would be punished in some way.

So, as I prayed for the third time, I beat my head against the door very lightly. It was little more than three light taps which were barely audible. It didn't hurt at all so I was doubtful that it would work.

To my surprise, Saint Quentin answered my prayer immediately.

I glimpsed the saint out of the corner of my eye. To be precise, I glimpsed his long hairy arm as it stretched over my shoulder, the fingers grasping a key.

The hand, arm and key were hardly visible. They had no colour either and were grey and transparent. But there was a definite click as the key entered the lock and twisted. As the saint faded away, I came to my feet, turned the handle and the door yielded.

The moment I could see beyond the door, my heart sank.

The giant was outside. He'd been waiting there all along.

The thin giant was sitting on the floor cross-legged, facing the door. Even in that position, his knees were higher than my head. His hood was pulled back so that his whole face was now visible. It was long and thin, the chin extremely elongated, but despite that it had a kindly expression and the brown eyes were filled with intelligence.

'Sit!' he commanded, gesturing towards the floor with the palm of his right hand facing downwards. Once again, his voice was soft but demanded instant obedience.

I obeyed and faced him. The silence lengthened.

'I believe your name to be Wulf, a shortened form of your full title – Brother Beowulf.'

I gazed at him in astonishment. How did he know my name?

'So I will address you as Wulf,' he continued. 'You may call me Hrothgar. I heard you praying. Do you think that your prayer was answered?'

There was no point in lying. He had been listening to me. He knew exactly what had happened.

'Yes, it was answered. I prayed to Saint Quentin, the patron saint of locksmiths. He unlocked the door for me.'

'Something opened the door for you, Wulf, but it wasn't Saint Quentin. You opened the door with your imagination.'

I didn't reply. I felt my jaw drop in astonishment. Then I felt fear. I remembered what the Abbot had once said to me when he reprimanded me for writing accounts of my life in the abbey rather than just copying books as we were supposed to do:

'Brother Halsall has caught you creating your own narratives. Writing your own stories – such sin! Do you not know that such works of the imagination must eventually lead to irresistible

temptations? Imagination belongs to God. It is not for us poor humans to attempt to exercise that faculty.'

'You have great power within you,' continued the thin giant, 'but you must be trained to use it properly. You are like me. Some refer to us as "Tulpamancers" but I prefer the title "Tulpar". With the power of our minds we have the ability to create *tulpas*. Do you know what a tulpa is?'

I shook my head.

'A tulpa is a thought-form. With training it is possible to cause an entity created within your imagination to take on a physical form in the real world. If you were trained and developed your ability properly, you could create a Saint Quentin who would walk beside you and be a companion as you travelled. So, do you wish me to train you?'

'I'd rather you allowed me to leave this underworld,' I replied. 'Your servant broke the leg of my master, Spook Johnson. He needs help. If he doesn't get it, he could die.'

'You needn't worry about your master. He is already safe and is being cared for. I am your master now – at least for a little while. I have asked you to decide, but in truth you cannot really refuse what I'm proposing. Becoming a tulpar is dangerous and may cause your death. But without training you will die anyway. The process will last for a few months at the most. After that, if you survive, you will be free to return to whatever life you wish to lead. Do you understand?'

'Just a few months? It would take so little time to train me?' I asked. To be trained as a spook took five years.

'It would just give you the rudiments of what you need and the ability to survive your own power. Much of what we do must, of necessity, be self-taught. But if you wished, you could return at a later date and I would train you to a higher level – but that would be your choice. Now come with me – there are things I wish to show you . . .'

He came to his feet, towering over me. I stood up too and meekly followed him to the front door of the mansion. Once outside, he led me directly to where the abhuman was still kneeling. It was perfectly still and didn't seem to be breathing.

'Is your creature dead?' I asked, starting to shiver. The air was cold; the temperature couldn't have been much above freezing.

The thin giant shook his head. 'No – it is suspended between life and death. Its heart does not beat and it does not breathe, but if I called its name life would surge within it and it would rise to its feet and do my bidding. This is a tulpa created from my imagination to walk in the world. In time you may be able to do the same.'

I shuddered. Even if I could, would I want to do such a thing? It seemed extremely cruel to create such a creature just to be a servant.

'Is it aware that it's a tulpa?' I asked.

'It must *never* know what it is. It believes it is an abhuman and that I saved it from death when it was badly injured. The moment that it realizes its true nature, it will collapse back into the dust, bone and blood from which it was created. That is very important, so commit it to memory – a tulpa must *never* know what it is. However, there is one type of tulpa to which that rule does not apply. We call it a "bound tulpa" but that is something to consider in the future. It need not concern you at present. Now follow me to the bridge. There is something vital that I must explain to you.'

The thin giant led me down the path between the two halves of the sunken lawn. At last we were standing together at the centre of the bridge, staring towards the trees. He pointed down at the water of the moat which was coloured red by the baleful sky. It looked like blood.

'Everything within the boundary of the moat is protected from the monsters that lurk in the forest. But were you to cross it and enter the trees alone you would be slain and devoured. Only the presence of my servant kept you safe as you passed through that forest yesterday. Listen! You can hear them.'

I listened and I certainly could hear disturbing noises. There were rustlings and the occasional breaking of branches. Some areas of vegetation seemed to be moving as if displaced by large creatures. Then I heard a deep bellow – a sound from some large animal that I could not place.

Although I couldn't see anything, I *knew* they were there. And they were powerful.

'Savage monstrous beasts guard my domain,' said Hrothgar.

Kratch the boggart guarded Tom Ward's house and garden and would rip into pieces anyone who trespassed there. It seemed to me that these beasts would probably be just as dangerous.

'They are tulpas that I have created for that purpose,' he continued. 'Never cross the water and enter the trees or you will perish. Now I will take you to my *Temple of Dreams*. Follow me!'

'What's a temple of dreams?' I asked.

'It's a special room where dream experiments are carried out,' he replied. 'It's a place where you may exercise your imagination. In that place you must also learn to control it. If you fail to do that, you will die.'

8

THE KITTEN

The room that Hrothgar had called his Temple of Dreams was small and sparsely furnished. The plaster walls were painted matt black and the bare floorboards, the same colour, were highly polished.

There were no windows in the room and opposite the door were the only two items of furniture. There was a table, upon it a saucer, the flickering stump of a candle and a small brown earthen jug. Beside the table was an upright wooden chair. Then I noticed a small wicker basket beneath the table.

The thin giant indicated the basket with his long bony finger. 'Place the basket in the centre of the room and remove the lid,' he commanded.

I knelt and lifted the basket. It weighed little. Then I carried it to the centre of the room just as he had instructed.

As I removed the lid, I heard a scratching within it and my heart began to beat faster, driven by fear. It reminded me of the noises that I sometimes heard under my bed.

There was a creature with claws inside the basket!

I stepped back in alarm and immediately felt foolish as a small black and white kitten leaped out of the basket and began to run around the room at great speed. It seemed no older than six weeks or so.

It ran towards me and using its claws climbed straight up my breeches and onto my shoulder. It brought a smile to my face but when I tried to stroke it, the kitten ran down my other leg to continue its frantic circling of the room.

'It likes you,' said Hrothgar with a smile. 'Do you like it in return?'

I shrugged. 'I've always liked kittens. We had lots of cats when I was a child. This one is very young, hardly old enough to have been weaned from its mother.'

'It had no mother. The creature is a tulpa that I created especially for your first lesson,' he told me.

I looked at the kitten in astonishment. I found it hard to believe that he had made that little creature, so full of life. But I didn't doubt him. After all I had seen the abhuman and heard his monstrous creatures moving within the trees.

'Note the candle!' the thin giant commanded. 'In less than an hour it will gutter and die. Whilst that flame flickers the kitten will live sustained by my imagination. When the candle goes out the kitten will fade with the flame – unless you can keep it alive!'

Horrified, I looked up at him. 'How will I do that?' I asked.

'Believe in the little animal. Believe that you can keep it alive. Believe in yourself. Feed it. Care for it. Above all use your imagination!'

He smiled and pointed towards the jug.

'That contains milk – feeding the kitten will help to bind it to you. I will leave you now and return later to see what you have achieved.'

Then Hrothgar walked out, leaving me alone with the kitten. I didn't hear him lock the door. What was to stop me from leaving the room? I supposed that even if I got clear of his dwelling, there was still the forest beyond the bridge full of beasts who would devour me.

As for what the thin giant had asked me to do, my feelings were mixed. I didn't want the kitten to die – but it wasn't a kitten, I told myself. It was a tulpa created by Devil magic.

No sooner had I thought that than the kitten began to rub its side against my right boot and purr very loudly. It wasn't the little creature's fault. It didn't know that it was a tulpa.

I bent down and gently stroked its head and back. Then I walked over to the table, lifted the jug and poured some of the milk into the saucer. No sooner had I placed it on the floor than the kitten started to lap at it noisily.

It didn't take it long to lick the saucer clean so I refilled it and the kitten began to lap the milk again even more furiously than the first time. I glanced at the candle.

It wouldn't be long before it guttered out.

I walked over to the chair, sat down and watched the kitten continuing to feed energetically. I knew that I couldn't just let it die. I had to try my very best to save it. At that moment the kitten finished the milk, ran towards me and jumped up onto my knee. It made three circuits following its tail before settling down. I stroked it until the little creature began to purr loudly.

Soon it seemed to be asleep. I kept glancing anxiously at the flickering candle.

All too soon the candle guttered and died, plunging the room into gloom. By now Hrothgar would no longer be sustaining its life force. I stroked the kitten and concentrated on attempting to will it to live.

It still seemed to be breathing but then, to my dismay, it began to whimper. I tried even harder but it did no good. Soon the kitten was taking huge rasping breaths, desperately trying to get air into its lungs. I tried to imagine it alive and well running up my breeches onto my shoulder again.

But its body convulsed and it lay still.

It was dead.

Then, to my astonishment, it slowly faded away and disappeared.

I sat there for a long time, thinking about what had happened. I felt sad but I had done my best. Hrothgar had created it out of nothing and now it had returned to that state. Then I looked up as the door opened and the thin giant walked into the room.

'That wasn't bad for a first attempt,' Hrothgar said, looking down at me. 'You extended its life by almost two minutes. I'm sure you'll do better next time. You must be hungry. Come with me and we'll eat together.'

After what I'd just witnessed, I had no appetite at all but I was glad to follow Hrothgar out of that room where the kitten had died whilst I had watched helplessly. He led me through another door into a much larger space where there were two tables and two chairs. One was normal – suited to the average human; the other was designed for the giant. Each table was furnished with a white plate with a knife and fork surrounded by dishes of steaming meat and vegetables.

As I sat down, I inhaled the delicious aroma of the food and my appetite returned immediately.

'Help yourself!' the giant invited me, beginning to spoon food onto his own plate which in diameter was at least twice that of my own.

I heaped carrots, potatoes and slices of lamb onto my plate and began to eat. It was delicious and the meat was really tender. It seemed ages since I'd eaten my last hot meal back at Tom Ward's Chipenden house.

'The food is excellent – very tasty. Did you cook it yourself?' I asked, trying to be polite and make conversation.

Hrothgar smiled and shook his head. 'I have a number of servants, each one specializing in a certain role. One is an excellent cook. Her name is Veronica.'

'Is she a tulpa?' I asked.

He nodded. 'Yes, but of course she doesn't know that's the case. But she's happy at her work and lives a comfortable life here. Feel free to ask questions. I am ready to satisfy your curiosity . . .'

I hesitated about satisfying my curiosity with regard to one thing in particular. But after a few moments of eating together in silence, I blurted it out.

'Are you human? I hope you don't mind me asking that but I've never seen anyone anywhere near your height. You are astonishingly tall!'

The thin giant had a strange expression on his face which was hard to read. Was it sadness or some painful memory? 'Yes, I am human and very mortal,' he explained, 'and I do not expect to live more than a few more years at the most. I have a disease that first became apparent about the time I reached thirty. I continued to grow unchecked. That growth still goes on and soon my heart will no longer be strong enough to maintain this enormous body. For me, time is short.'

'I'm sorry,' I mumbled, sorry that I'd mentioned it.

'Don't be. It is something over which neither of us has any control. What must be, must be. Now, I would like to ask *you* a question, if I may – the small red feather which I returned to you provides a powerful protection against the magic of an enemy. Who threatens you?'

I hesitated. We were in an underworld, a place between the dark and the human world. Could I trust this giant? For all I knew he could be an ally of Circe.

He saw my reluctance to answer and shrugged his huge shoulders. 'In time, when you feel it is right, tell me who your enemy is – I may just be able to help. Now I will ask you another question. I took a mirror from you and I have not yet returned it. Why do you carry such an object? Is it vanity?' he asked with a smile.

I shook my head but said nothing.

'Then perhaps it is for purposes of communication? Am I right?'

Once again, I did not reply.

'It is your choice to withhold that information and I respect your decision. I returned the feather to keep you from danger but I am sorry to say that I will not return the mirror and the dagger until you are ready to leave my domain. And now, if you have eaten your fill, we will continue your training . . .'

I followed him back to the Temple. The basket was under the table again. A stump of a fresh candle was burning on the table next to the saucer and jug.

'Move the basket into the centre of the room and we will try again,' he said.

I obeyed and then removed the lid without being asked. Almost immediately, a small kitten leaped out and began to circle the room furiously. It was black and white like the previous one, but this time it didn't run up my breeches and onto my shoulder.

'It looks exactly like the other one,' I told him.

'It's the same kitten,' Hrothgar told me.

'You brought it back to life? Will it remember being here? Will it remember me?'

He nodded and then shrugged. 'Perhaps, but that's not important. I'll leave you now. See if you can improve on your previous effort . . .'

I didn't agree but I didn't bother to argue. I didn't like the idea of the kitten remembering its own death. If so, would it realize what was happening when it began to feel the same way again?

Hrothgar left the room and I tried again to save the life of the kitten.

I tried. I really tried. I couldn't have done more. I fed the kitten, sat it on my knee and stroked it until it purred. I spoke nonsense to it, trying to comfort it with my voice. I willed it to live with all the strength of imagination that I could muster.

It all came to nothing.

The candle went out and the kitten died soon afterwards.

9

Something Under My Bed

No sooner had the dead kitten vanished than the door opened and the thin giant re-entered the room.

Hrothgar gave me the faintest of smiles. 'It lived slightly longer than last time but I think you are tired. You should return to your bedroom and get some sleep.'

I wondered how he knew how long the kitten had survived. After all, he hadn't been here watching. But I did feel tired and didn't need the suggestion to be made twice. Hrothgar left me at my bedroom door and this time, after he had closed it, I didn't hear the key turning in the lock.

Although locking me in was no longer needed, I was still a prisoner, and I shuddered at the thought of the unseen monsters moving through the trees. I removed my boots again and left them by the door. The bed had been made and everything was tidy.

I washed at the basin but, before undressing and climbing into bed, I glanced through the lower window again. The abhuman was still kneeling in exactly the same position and the sky still glimmered that same baleful red. The sun would never rise here, the view outside of my window never changed, and there was no easy way to measure the passage of time.

How long had I been awake? It was impossible to say. It certainly didn't feel that a morning, afternoon and evening had passed, yet I felt as tired as if I'd endured a long full exhausting day. Time moved strangely here.

I blew out the candle and climbed into bed. It was warm and comfortable. I fell asleep very quickly.

I awoke just as rapidly.

I could hear something scratching under my bed.

I felt a jolt of fear, but when I listened carefully there was only silence. Had I really heard scratching? Or was that scary sound just the remnant of a nightmare that I had already forgotten?

The place between waking and sleeping was strange. Sometimes a nightmare could follow you back so that you lay awake sweating and fearful for quite some time.

The silence continued and gradually I began to relax. My heart began to slow. I was still tired and felt myself pleasantly drifting off to sleep. But then the scratching began again. This time there was no mistaking it. I couldn't pretend it was just the remnant of a dream. This was real. There was something under my bed scratching at the floorboards.

My sleepiness fled. It was replaced by terror.

When I'd first heard that scratching in the millhouse, Spook Johnson had laughed at my fears. Then I had heard it at Chipenden and now wished that I'd mentioned it to Alice. This house was the third location where I had been haunted by it. The thing had the power to follow me, to reach me wherever I was, even into the underworld.

I lay there in that absolute darkness. I wished I hadn't blown out the candle. In order to light it again, I would have to get out of bed and walk over to the table but I was too afraid to do that. I imagined getting out of bed and a cold clawed hand reaching out from beneath it to grab my ankle.

I began to pray to Andrew, the patron saint of those who were haunted by demons. To be truthful, Brother Halsall at the abbey had in fact said that he was the patron saint of singers and fishermen. Halsall trained the noviciates at the monastery and considered himself to be something of an expert regarding saints. But an old monk called Filbert had once told me that Andrew was capable of dealing with demonic entities – though most other monks thought Filbert a little mad.

I prayed hard for about two minutes but there was no response and the scratching became louder. I thought about what the thin giant had told me – that I was not receiving help from the saints but generating aid through the power of my imagination. I was still not totally convinced of that. Even if it was true, my prayers certainly aided my imagination and helped to make each saint who responded become manifest to some degree.

So I continued to pray but it didn't help. The scratching became more frantic as if the thing under the bed was trying to claw its way down through the floorboards. That made me think. Why would it do that? That would take it further away from me. Was it trying to escape? Whatever it was, maybe it wasn't a threat to me after all?

Then I realized that I'd been stupid in thinking that. There was another much more likely terrifying possibility. What if the thing was actually *under* the floorboards, clawing its way upwards to emerge under my bed?

All was silent again. All I could hear was my breathing and the thundering of my heart.

Then after a few moments the scratching began again. I wondered where the thin giant slept. Surely he had heard that commotion and would come to investigate?

I'd thought things were bad enough, but suddenly they got much worse. The scratching stopped but then there was a sudden change. The whole bed began to shake as if it had been seized by a pair of gigantic hands. Then it began to rock from side to side until that movement became even more extreme. The bed rose up into the air before crashing down onto the floorboards. This happened three times as I lay there terrified, afraid that I might be hurled to the floor.

Now there was another sound, another movement. I could feel something slowly slithering across the top of the bed towards me. I could hear the faint rasp of friction against the blanket which covered me.

Then my heart leaped into my throat as a rough hand suddenly gripped my right wrist!

I tried to pull it free but the fingers were cold as ice and as strong as steel. And I could see the hand that gripped me because it was glowing slightly, a sickly yellow and green. It was covered in warts, each one tufted with hair. It had six long fingers and a fat thumb, each tipped with a long sharp talon. Beyond the hand I could see the impossibly long thin hairy arm to which it was attached: an arm which extended across the blanket, down the side of the bed and then beneath it.

The hand began to pull me, dragging me across the bed. Desperately, I grabbed the far edge of the bed with my left hand. But it delayed my movement by less than a second. My hand came away clutching the undersheet and then I was jerked out of the bed with force, hit the floor hard and lay on my back momentarily stunned.

Then, still gripped by the taloned hand, I was dragged across the floorboards towards the bed. The area beneath it was glowing a green and yellow, and by that baleful illumination, I saw a scene straight from Hell.

Directly under the bed there was a dark hole in the floorboards. Was it a doorway to the dark, a gateway to Hell itself? From that hole the long hairy arm protruded. There must be some fearsome beast hidden within that darkness. But for the arm and taloned hand, all I could see of it was two large red eyes glowing like orbs of fire.

What form the Devil-beast took I hardly dared to think, but I could hear a harsh grating noise like sharp hungry teeth being ground together and imagined a terrible large fanged mouth ready to devour me. As the hand dragged me towards the pit, I grabbed again at the edge of the bed but missed and all my attempts to resist came to nothing. Within seconds I would be pulled down into that hole, the lair of the beast.

I shouted then as loudly as I could. 'Help me! Help me! Please help me!'

But I knew it was too late. I was already beyond help. I was about to experience a terrible painful death – and after that even my soul would be in jeopardy.

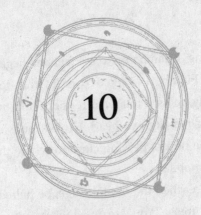

10

WULF'S BANE

My head was almost under the bed then and I had been dragged very close to the dark hole. I'd almost given up struggling when I heard a tremendous crash from behind me. It sounded like the bedroom door had been flung open with force to crash back against the wall.

Then a loud voice boomed out: 'Avaunt! Begone!'

To my relief the grip on my wrist loosened and then I was released. The hand and arm slithered away like a snake and vanished into the hole.

'You've made a terrible mess of the bedroom floor!' commented a voice, now hardly louder than a whisper.

I looked up and saw the thin giant standing over me.

'I didn't do it—' I began to say, but Hrothgar cut me off with a curt 'Yes you did! Who else could be responsible? Get to your feet, dress yourself and follow me!'

Still shaking, I clambered to my feet and began to pull on my clothes. Finally, I walked over to the doorway and tugged on my boots. I followed him out into the darkness, the menacing red sky overhead. He led the way down the path from the house, passing close to where the abhuman still knelt immobile.

When we reached the small bridge, he halted and stared towards the trees. 'You are in a worse situation than I thought,' he observed. 'It has reached a crisis already.'

'What has? I don't understand . . .'

'Have you heard noises under your bed previously?' he asked.

'A few times there have been strange scratching sounds. It happened at various locations. But nothing like that!' I exclaimed, aware that I was still trembling. I remembered the horror of the grasping taloned hand and the dark pit beneath my bed. 'Is it a demon that haunts me?'

The thin giant shook his head. 'It is something that you have unwittingly created with your own powerful imagination. It is what I warned you about and partly why I brought you here. Because of what we are we initially pose a danger to ourselves. In fact, we have a name for that self-inflicted threat – we call it *Tulpar's Bane*. The creativity that can create tulpas to do our bidding can also, unfortunately, create ones that could destroy us. I hoped to have more time to train you but the danger has come far sooner than I expected.'

'Then what can I do?' I asked.

'The easier way is gone. You are too late to embrace it and modify that dangerous tulpa into something that is no longer a threat. So now it must be the other – the *Path of Blood*. You must create a tulpa that will defend you against the threat and exterminate it. And you must do it quickly.'

I shook my head in despair. 'How am I supposed to manage that? I can't even keep a kitten alive for longer than a few minutes.'

'Yes, but it was *my* tulpa that you tried to keep alive. It is difficult to do that with another's creation. That was a challenging exercise that I gave you – firstly, to test you, and also to build up your strength. A tulpa that you create yourself will be much easier to maintain. Come with me.'

I followed him back to the house. Once inside he took me into the room that he called the Temple of Dreams.

'The easier method is called the *Path of Peace*. Using that, you would have gradually transformed that dangerous tulpa under your bed into a benign friend,' Hrothgar explained. 'But that is a slow process and it is far too late for that. Now you must destroy it before it destroys you. You used a tulpa to open the locked door to your room. Am I correct in surmising that other tulpas, partly beyond your control, have also manifested themselves to you? No doubt you thought that you used prayer. Which of them might be able to defend you and eventually destroy that which seeks to kill you?'

It didn't take me long to work that out.

'His name is Raphael,' I told Hrothgar. Then I explained that I'd thought him to be a saint with wings and a sword. I told him how it must have been Raphael who had saved me from the marsh water witch, even though my master had thought it a large white bird.

'Then that is the tulpa you must seek to control,' he told me. 'Raphael need not be a companion but he must persist just long enough to deal with that which threatens you. And he must come when you call. He must be trained to obey you promptly. An attack might manifest itself suddenly.'

'But that's what I find really hard. Sometimes Raphael doesn't respond at all . . .'

'You must *make* him attend. If he does not answer your call, you will be destroyed. Firstly, you must create him within your imagination. You must practise until he is there, vivid and in great detail. Then, call his name. Summon him. When you open your eyes, he will be before you. Have faith in yourself, Wulf. Believe that you can do it! The threat that you face comes to all trainee tulpars and yet it is very personal – something straight from your own imagination. The true name of what you face is *Wulf's Bane*. You must destroy that entity or die.'

Hrothgar left me then and I felt close to despair. He made it seem so easy but I was anything but confident. However,

I had to try because my life depended on it so I sat at the table, closed my eyes and tried to visualize Raphael.

I started by imagining his huge white-feathered wings and extended the image until I saw his body dressed in a bright blue robe. He looked well built and powerful, like he would be a match for the monster. I'd not personally seen an image of a muscular saint – but who was to say that they weren't? Next, I added a black leather belt and boots. His face was difficult for me to see. Whenever he'd appeared to me before, he'd been blurred so I started with his long hair which I imagined to be gleaming like gold. I was still unable to give his face form but then I had a moment of inspiration.

There was a row of stained-glass windows in the abbey. Each featured the head and shoulders of a haloed saint. One of them was Saint Raphael. I brought my memory of the window into my mind and concentrated until I could see the blue eyes, the aquiline nose and the strong jaw.

I had him to perfection!

I held the image fully realized, gleaming before me in my imagination.

But when I opened my eyes the room was empty.

That night, I retired to my bedroom in fear. After many failed attempts, I had managed to materialize the tulpa just twice. And the second time it had taken him long minutes to arrive, sufficient time for me to have been dragged into the hole there to be savaged, chewed thoroughly and eaten. But not only that, Raphael had been pale, grey and insubstantial – not suited to dealing with the all too strong and solid form of the hungry horrific monster under my bed.

Forcing myself to be brave, I peered under the bed and was disturbed to see the ruin of the floor and the dark threatening hole. I suppose I'd expected it to be repaired, that one of Hrothgar's tulpa servants might have fixed the wooden boards. But what was the point when it was certain to happen again? I realized also that I might not get the warning of the previous night. There would be no clawing and scratching because the hole was already there.

This time I did not blow out the candle. I could not bear for the room to be cloaked in darkness. I climbed into bed full of terrible anticipation.

I lay there for a long time too fearful to close my eyes. Then I heard noises under the bed. This time they were different. As I expected, there was no scratching of talons. Instead of that, there was a sucking slurping sound as if something was dragging itself upwards through the soft earth beneath the floor. Then there was a pause before the scariest noise of all began. By the flickering candlelight I saw the taloned hand and long arm slithering towards me across the sheets.

'Raphael!' I called out in terror. 'Come to my aid!'

There was no response from my tulpa. The talons gripped my wrist and began to drag me across the bed. But then

Raphael did appear. He looked insubstantial, hardly more than a shimmering translucence. But I could see his shape, the great wings folded at his back, and he carried a huge sword which he gripped with both hands.

When he struck downwards with that sword I had a brief moment of hope. But the blade of the sword passed through the long hairy arm without doing any damage.

Then Raphael faded away and the monster tulpa jerked me from the bed onto the floor.

My bane was about to slay me.

It was then that the door burst open.

'Avaunt! Begone!' Hrothgar cried.

The thin giant had saved me again.

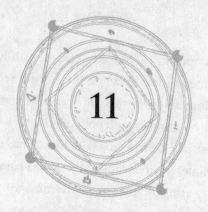

11

GRISTLES AND WRAITHS

It took a month before I could materialize the winged tulpa fully. The problem was that Raphael did not always appear promptly, so it was that Hrothgar had needed to rescue me on five more occasions.

Whether he waited outside the door listening for my cries of fear, or just came from his own room warned by some magical means when I was in danger, I do not know. But arrive he did and always just in time to save me.

The times when the monster tulpa did not appear were hardly much better. I slept little. Always there was the terrible anticipation of the noises under my bed that would warn of an imminent attack.

Then, just when I believed that things couldn't get worse, they did.

'I have to go away for a time,' Hrothgar told me. 'Work even harder at your craft. Whilst I am away there will be nobody here to save you. Now, you must save yourself.'

I felt hurt that he was about to abandon me. His words seemed harsh and cruel but I didn't protest. I just watched Hrothgar leave the underworld, cross the bridge and enter the trees. He never once glanced back.

During the long hours whilst I was awake, I was in dread of the time when I must retire to my bed and face my bane – the entity I had created inadvertently. But then I had a moment of inspiration. I would not go to bed and await the coming of the thing from the dark hole beneath it. I would spend the hours when I normally slept in the Temple of Dreams. And, if possible, I would not allow myself to sleep.

Too nervous to bother with supper, I went there immediately and lit five candles, placing three of them on the table and one each side of the door. That made the room bright enough to dispel a little of my fear. Then I pulled the chair away from the table and placed it in the centre of the room. This was better than lying in bed in dread of what lurked beneath it. And if the beast tulpa emerged from the earth below, it would first have to scratch its way through the boards of this room and I would receive ample warning of its arrival.

Although this was the time when I usually slept, I didn't feel in the slightest bit tired. My heart was beating fast and I was filled with a terrible anticipation.

I did not have long to wait . . .

The attack built slowly, beginning with terrifying intimidating sounds.

There were hard threatening thumps against the floorboards. They began in the far corner of the room nearest to the door. Then they switched in less than a second to the corner opposite. How could the thing move so quickly?

The tulpa explored each corner of the room at least twice and then moved its attention to the centre directly under my chair. Then the scratching began, the hard, insistent abrasion of talons against wood.

I had thought it would somehow be better in this temple, far better than the terror of having something emerge from under your bed. But now I realized it was just as bad. Soon the taloned hand would emerge to seize me and drag me down into the creature's lair.

In a panic, I lurched to my feet and carried my chair to the wall, as far away as possible from where the monster was scratching its way up through the floorboards. Then I sat there trembling with fear, waiting for the hand to gouge its way to the surface.

It didn't take long. The hand with its six fingers and the broad thumb emerged as far as the wrist and then paused. The talons looked very sharp, capable of slicing through flesh like a barber's razor. That hand seemed to sense exactly where I was sitting. It began to slither across the floorboards directly towards me, the long hairy wart-encrusted arm extending behind it.

I didn't move but it was the signal for me to summon Raphael. I concentrated, then called his name aloud.

'Raphael! Raphael! Defend me against this demon!'

The tulpa saint began to take shape. At first, to my dismay, it lacked colour and I could see right through the wings and upper body. I remembered how it had cut at the arm of the monster but the sword had passed through it without effect, the blade having no substance. Surely that wasn't going to happen again after I'd worked so hard?

But then my tulpa suddenly took on a gleaming solidity. Raphael was hovering close to the ceiling, maintaining that position with slow steady beats of his huge white-feathered wings. His body was dressed in a brilliant blue robe and he held his sword aloft, his face exactly as I had copied it from the stained-glass window in the abbey, the aquiline nose, strong jaw, and blue eyes filled with determination.

As the hand slithered beneath him, Raphael brought the sword down with great speed and force. The monster screamed as the sword cut through the wrist, embedding itself in the floorboards. For the first time I began to feel that I might survive.

Then Raphael tugged the blade free and, with two rapid beats of his wings, flew across the room and positioned himself directly above the hole from which the hand had emerged.

Then a really strange thing happened. It was something totally unexpected. It only lasted maybe a few seconds at the most but suddenly I was looking through the eyes of Raphael.

I could feel the weapon in my hands and I gazed down into the hole to see my bane, the red-eyed long-fanged monster, staring up at me.

I was two people momentarily joined as one. I could sense the determination and the fearlessness in the tulpa; I was aware of my own terror too. But gradually that fear lessened as I seemed to draw courage from my creation.

I stabbed twice downwards with the point of the sword right between the creature's eyes. As I sliced downwards, terrible high-pitched screams came from the monster's lair to echo from wall to wall.

Then I was back in my own body and a fountain of blood was spurting up through the hole and surging across the floor towards me. That lasted just a few moments. Very suddenly Raphael was gone and the blood-tide vanished along with the severed hand and long hairy arm. All that remained was the hole and a patch of damp sawdust surrounding it.

I came to my feet very slowly, my knees trembling. I felt elated because I'd finally succeeded. I was free of the threat that had threatened to end my life prematurely. Or at least I hoped so. Surely the monster wouldn't return another night?

It was at that moment that the door opened and Hrothgar walked into the room shaking his head.

'That's another fine mess you've made, Wulf! Do you intend to destroy every floor in my house?' he demanded. Then he smiled and stepped forward and patted me on the shoulder. 'You must be hungry,' he said. 'Let's go and eat.'

We ate in the kitchen. I waited in silence, sitting at the table, whilst Hrothgar prepared and cooked a light meal of fish cakes and carrot slices.

At first we ate without speaking, but then I started to question him. 'You never really went away, did you?' I asked. 'You were always close by.'

'Of course I was. It was important for you to think that you were alone and your survival depended upon what you did for yourself. That brought things to a crisis and made you reach deep inside yourself for all the strength you could muster. I thought you would survive and I was right. But, just in case things went wrong, I was standing by ready to intervene.'

'Thanks for that. Without your training I would have died. But tell me – is it really over? The monster won't come back, will it?'

Hrothgar smiled reassuringly. 'I promise you that it is over. All of us face that crisis early in our development. You have destroyed your bane and passed beyond it and now can begin to develop your skills further.'

Then I thought of something else. 'For a second or so, I thought I was looking through the eyes of my tulpa. I could feel the sword in my hands too as I stabbed it down into the hole to kill the monster . . .'

Hrothgar stared hard into my eyes for a few moments without speaking. Then he shrugged and carried on eating.

'Did that really happen?' I asked.

'Perhaps in the stress of the moment you thought it did. Or maybe you really were looking through the eyes of your tulpa. Such a thing is very rare and only happens to a few of us. A splinter of your soul enters your creation and it becomes . . . well, we shall see. It is linked to what I once mentioned to you – the creation of *bound tulpas*. Time will show us your full capabilities. I hope you will stay with me longer. You have much to learn and the bulk of it you will discover for yourself. But this is a safe environment for you, Wulf, and your progress will be smoother and faster here.'

I didn't reply. I was thinking of the world that I had left behind – of the danger from Circe posed to Tom and Alice and their child, Tilda. I was also concerned for my injured master, Will Johnson, who had been training me as a spook's apprentice.

'How is Spook Johnson now?' I asked. 'Your servant deliberately broke his leg. I thought that was cruel.'

'Yes. I knew that it would be necessary. I had watched Johnson and knew what kind of man he was. Your master is strong and stubborn and I predicted that he would not easily be deterred. So damaging his mobility was the easiest option. Besides, in the long term I believe it might be good for him. Each one of us has a limited time on this earth and we must use it to develop and grow. He will no longer be the same man with the same strength and he will have to come to terms with that. He may not do so. But if he can, Spook Johnson will be a far better person. We can but hope. At the moment he is coping and is back practising his trade as a spook.'

'That's good,' I told Hrothgar, but I was not totally put at ease. I knew that Johnson had always delighted in his strength and fighting skill and would find it hard to deal with having to accept that his prowess might be limited in any way.

One part of me wanted to return to the outer world and visit Tom, Alice and Will Johnson, but I knew I still had a lot to learn. If I trained, I might be more use in the fight against Circe. So I decided to stay with Hrothgar for a little while longer.

*

I spent a lot of time in my room reading books that Hrothgar brought to me but there was a day when he took me to a gloomy room that I hadn't seen before. It was windowless and dank.

'Within this room,' explained Hrothgar, 'are the means to make permanent tulpas that, like my servants, never disappear. Once created, minimal effort of will is required to maintain them.'

There were four large mounds on the stone floor and each contained something different – desiccated plants, dry soil, sand and small fragments of bone. Beside them was a large pail containing a dark liquid which gave off a strong metallic smell. I guessed that it contained the blood of an animal.

Hrothgar pointed to the heap of bones. 'There's cartilage as well as bones there. Another name for cartilage is gristle and that's the name we give to the tulpas that I make here. The abhuman, Mother Martha, my cook Veronica and the others are all what I call "gristles" . . .

'Some of us prefer not to go down this path,' he continued. 'Without using these substances as an anchor, it is still possible to create tulpas that will persist for many hours at a time, sometimes even days. I call those "wraiths" and although at times they can be pale and unsubstantial, more like ghosts than things of flesh and blood, they can also be solid and hard to distinguish from creatures born into this world. The monster under your bed was solid enough, as was your tulpa Raphael that put an end to it. The kitten was also a wraith.'

I didn't like the idea of using plant material and certainly not blood and those pieces of bone. It reminded me too much of the practices of dark magic. It was what some witches did, especially using bone and blood they had taken – the first usually from graveyards, the second from living people who did not survive the encounter. I didn't think using them was a price worth paying to make a tulpa persist. So I told Hrothgar that and explained why.

He didn't seem concerned. 'It is your decision, Wulf. Each of us must use the means that make us comfortable. It is always better not to come into conflict with one's own conscience – and certainly not override it or let it be overridden . . .'

As he finishing speaking, a strange expression came over his long face and I swore his lips trembled for a few seconds after uttering those final words. I couldn't say for certain what emotion had disturbed him or what lay behind it, but it reminded me of the faces of people who came to repent for their sins at the monastery. Hrothgar looked guilty. I didn't feel it was my place to remark upon it, so behaved as if I hadn't noticed anything.

He said no more about gristles or wraiths, though I wondered if he was a little disappointed in me. But he was still friendly and helpful and continued to offer me advice.

He also taught me mental techniques designed to aid drawing upon my creativity to form a tulpa. The best one involved deep slow breathing and counting down from five to zero, at which point I had to breathe out with force and hurl my will into the act of creation.

I practised it over and over again until that technique became second nature to me.

But the outer world was calling me more strongly each day. Eventually, I could no longer resist that call and decided I must leave.

When I told Hrothgar my decision to leave, he accepted it without argument and soon the time came to say our farewells.

'This is food for the journey, cheese and bread. And here are the things that I took from you when you first entered my house,' he said, handing me the knife and the mirror that Alice had given to me. He didn't mention the two items again or ask me questions about them. Neither did Hrothgar refer to the red feather that he'd allowed me to keep.

That surprised me more than anything because he'd once asked me before which enemy it kept at bay. I suddenly had an urge to confide in him. After all, he'd given me training that had saved my life.

'The feather is magical – it keeps my enemy, Circe, at bay!' I blurted out.

'Circe, the goddess?' he asked. It was a strange thing to say. It wasn't widely known that Circe was operating within the County.

'Yes,' I replied, staring at Hrothgar, who was no longer meeting my eyes.

'Who gave you the feather?' he asked. 'It must be someone with formidable magic.'

'Yes, the magic is powerful. I would have fallen into the clutches of the goddess already but for that feather.'

I did not give him Alice's name. A name was a very powerful thing and I'd learned to keep important ones secret, if I could help it. He had treated me well and I had no cause to doubt him, but suddenly I was on my guard again and an uncomfortable silence came between us.

Then he walked me to the bridge over the moat. 'If you decide to return for further training, you will be safe walking through the trees alone, Wulf. And you will be more than welcome. But do not leave it too long. I fear that my life is drawing to a close.'

I thanked him and walked into the trees. I could hear the huge beasts moving unseen, hidden by the foliage, but nothing approached me and soon I reached the two tall sycamores.

12

A DIFFERENT DWELLING

As I passed between the two trees, the red glare was replaced by blue sky and the noon sun, which was surprisingly warm. I walked on until I reached the fence round the cottage. I glimpsed a face peering through the front lace-curtained window. No doubt it was Mother Martha, watching me leave.

Then I noticed that there were no dead leaves on the ground and the ones in the trees were fresh and green.

When I'd entered the underworld, it had been very late autumn and most of the branches had been bare. The temperature of the air was much warmer than I remembered too and it seemed like early summer. I knew that time could sometimes pass at a different speed in an underworld but it always moved forward, not back. Did that mean that six months or more had passed in the outer world?

I walked faster and headed north. As I walked, I kept reliving inside my head all that had happened to me and I hardly noticed my progress. When, at last, I began to climb the steep hill towards Chipenden village, it was getting colder, the sun already very low over the distant waters of Morecambe Bay. As I entered the first cobbled street and passed the butcher's shop, I remembered the first time I'd visited here.

I had come to seek out Tom Ward and beg him to return to Salford with me to rescue Spook Johnson from the clutches of a witch. Much had happened since then.

Out of the corner of my eye I saw the butcher come out of the door behind and stride into the street. I kept walking and didn't glance back. I was in no mood for talking.

'Hey, boy! Don't I know you?' he called after me.

I halted and turned round and he walked towards me. 'Aye – I remember you now. I never forget a face, but you're a bit of a shrimp. You're no bigger than the last time I saw you. Trying to get help from the local spook, weren't you?'

He was a big man, so no doubt he thought it funny calling me a shrimp.

I nodded. 'Yes, and now I'm here to see Spook Ward again . . .'

'Well, I'm afraid you're out of luck, boy!' the butcher said, staring hard at me as if finding it hard to believe what he saw. 'Nobody's seen hide nor hair of him down in the village for many a long year and some folk are missing him badly. There are dark things abroad that need dealing with. Few villagers go out after sunset. And it's got so bad that the Bishop's Quisitor has taken refuge in Caster Castle and rarely ventures out.' He shook his head wearily. 'Of course, there are still patrols sent out from the castle but they do little good. They accuse innocent people of witchcraft and arrest a few of the poor wretches before disappearing back into their stronghold before sunset. So take care, especially after dark, and beware of that boggart because it's still loose in the garden without the Spook to keep it under control,' he continued whilst wiping his hands on his blood-stained apron. 'You'd be crazy to go anywhere near it . . .'

I nodded, turned and carried on walking. No sign of Tom Ward for years? That was unlikely. But fear clutched at my heart. I'd guessed that I'd been in the underworld almost a year. Could two or three years have actually passed? Or maybe it was just that Tom kept away from the village because of the military patrols from the castle?

The main street of Chipenden was almost deserted. A solitary old man was hobbling away from me supported by a walking stick; a woman clutching a shopping basket was trying to peer into the window of the grocer's shop which was boarded up. Some of the houses looked abandoned too. This was no longer a safe place to be.

I walked on quickly and took the path that led to the withy trees crossroad. I thought it would probably be safe enough to go straight to the garden as I'd spent time there before and the boggart should recognize me and not attack. But I didn't want to take the risk. It was best to ring the bell so that Tom could meet me down at the crossroads.

It was gloomy under the branches and tendrils of mist writhed amongst the trees like grey snakes. My memory once more conjured images from the recent past. I had rung the bell and a young hooded man had come in response. At first, I'd thought him too young to be a spook and considered him more likely to be an apprentice. But I'd been wrong. I'd been wrong so many times about Tom Ward and what his role as a spook entailed.

I approached the tree to which the bell was attached and reached up for the rope. Then I stepped back in puzzlement. The rope had gone and I saw something which dismayed me. The bell was lying on the ground half-covered with grass and weeds.

It might have been brought crashing to earth by a storm, but why wouldn't Tom fix it back into position? After all, it was the traditional method by which anyone requiring help could summon the Spook. That way they didn't need to approach the garden and risk the wrath of the boggart.

I set off up the hill walking towards the house. The higher I climbed the thicker the mist became until the visibility was down to just a few paces. It seemed to be getting colder too. This was a chilly evening for early summer. At last I came to the hedge that marked the boundary of the garden. There I paused and listened. Tom had once told me that the boggart gave three growls before it attacked intruders. So, even if it didn't recognize me, at least I'd get that warning.

Encouraged by the silence, I took three slow careful steps into the garden and paused again. Everything was still as quiet as a grave so I walked through the long grass of the lawn towards the Spook's house.

Then I could hear a sound – a faint whining in the distance. But it didn't sound anything like the roar of the boggart that I remembered.

The grass had been well tended the last time I'd visited, but now it was long and unkempt. It needed a scythe taking to it. Tom must be really busy to have let it grow so long. Then I noticed something else that brought me to a halt.

There were saplings and bushes growing in the lawn – and a lot of them. They should have been cut back as seedlings. I wondered if Tom had decided to allow this part of the garden to be filled with trees. One spindly sycamore sapling was already taller than I was. How could it have grown so quickly?

The mist was getting thicker and it was so cold that now I was shivering violently. At last I could see the big three-storey house rearing up before me. As I got closer, I immediately realized that there was something terribly wrong.

The back door was hanging open supported by a single hinge and the window next to it was broken. There were also saplings growing very close to the house, with weeds and grass hanging down from the gutters.

The house looked to be abandoned. But I found that hard to believe. Tom might be away on spook's business but he would never desert that house which had been used by spooks for generations.

I went in and noticed that Tom Ward's staff was leaning in the corner and his hooded gown was hanging from its usual hook, but it was covered in patches of mildew and it was damp and smelling of rot.

I walked into the front room and the table was set with plates and cutlery as if for a meal. But there was no fire in the grate and there were damp patches on the ceiling. The range of pots on the window ledge had once contained a profusion of verdant herbs; what remained was brown, black or grey, withered, dry and dead. What had been a warm and welcoming place was now cold, forbidding and clearly abandoned.

It seemed much colder here than it had been outdoors. I could see my breath steaming in the gloom.

What had happened? Why had Tom and Alice left their home?

There were two possibilities that I could hardly bear to consider. What if they'd been arrested by one of the two Quisitors working for the Bishop of Blackburn? Alice was a witch and the Church would view Tom as her associate and a servant of Hell. They would face imprisonment, torture and finally death by burning.

Then there was another possibility. What if, as Tom Ward had feared, Alice had tried to pit her magical strength against Circe and lost? Both Tom and Alice might have been slain. And what of Tilda, Alice's baby? Had the goddess finally claimed her? Or was she still under the protection of Grimalkin, the dead witch assassin? A year and a day she had promised Alice to keep the child safe from Circe and then make further provision if necessary. Yes, at least Tilda should be all right.

I walked to the door and gazed out over the garden. There was one thing that didn't make sense. Either of those two terrible fates could have befallen Tom and Alice but the neglected house and garden spoke of a duration of time much longer than several months. I didn't like to think about what that suggested.

I wondered what I should do now. Maybe they'd simply abandoned the house on hearing that the Quisitor knew where they lived? In that case, where would they have gone? The millhouse close to the canal was one possibility and Spook Johnson might still be working from there. Then there was a spook's house somewhere up on Anglezarke Moor – but I hadn't a clue where exactly that was to be found.

It was damp, and even colder inside the house than it was outdoors. As I thought it was likely to rain before morning and at least most of the roof provided shelter, I climbed the stairs towards the room that Tom and Alice usually gave me – it was the one used by all the apprentices who had trained in this house. I pushed open the green-painted door and stepped inside, to be pleasantly surprised.

It was gloomy inside but one glance told me that none of the panes in the sash window were broken and there was no sign of damp patches on the ceiling. The room felt slightly warmer than downstairs.

I felt the bed. It was a bit damp but that was only to be expected. Grass would be worse and the ground under it harder than this mattress. I didn't bother to get undressed, nor did I take my boots off. I just lay down and closed my eyes.

I was exhausted and fell asleep within a minute or two.

I awoke suddenly and sat up. It was pitch black in the room but I could still see someone standing at the foot of the bed. It was a woman and she was glowing with a soft yellow light. At first I thought it was a ghost – and it certainly was one of the deceased.

It was Grimalkin, the terrifying dead witch assassin.

13

I AM GRIMALKIN

I had last seen the witch assassin a few months earlier when
Alice had given Tilda to her. Once, Grimalkin had been an
ally of Tom and Alice but she had died fighting one of the
Old Gods and had fallen into Hell – the place that witches
called the dark. Tom had told me that she had the power to
visit the earth only between sunset and sunrise. One single
ray of sunlight would destroy her.

Grimalkin was more like a demon than a mortal. She
wore a necklace of white bones and there were straps across
her body holding sheathed blades. Her hair was dark and her
skirt was split, each half bound to a thigh, no doubt to give
her more freedom of movement when fighting. She had
been the designated killer of the Malkin clan and she looked
more than ready to deal out death now.

'Don't be afraid, child,' she said softly. 'I am Grimalkin but I will not harm you. You are in no danger from me.'

The words contradicted the threat that her open mouth revealed. I shuddered at two deadly rows of teeth that had been filed to points. They could rip out a throat with ease.

'When you were taken by the abhuman, Tom and Alice searched for you for many months,' she continued, 'and you appear to be no older. By now you should be a man. As you have not aged perceptibly you must have spent time in one of the underworlds. Which one? Where have you been hidden?'

Her words chilled me to the bone. I was now more afraid of what she was suggesting than Grimalkin herself. Everything was coming together now, the little touches of unease forming into a large terrifying truth: the butcher had called me a shrimp as if I were smaller than I should be, then he'd stared at me with a strange expression on his face; the bell that hadn't been replaced; the saplings sprouting from the lawn; and, finally, the abandoned house.

'How long is it since I was taken?' I asked, dreading Grimalkin's reply.

'Fourteen years,' she replied.

It was some while before I was able to speak. When I finally could, the witch assassin insisted that I tell her where I had been held and what had happened to me. When I'd finished my account, she explained the erratic passage of time in an underworld.

'Within an underworld time can move at a different speed than in the world outside. Sometimes, when a month or so is spent there, many years can pass in the outer world. The reverse sometimes occurs. You could spend a year in an underworld and leave it to find that only a few minutes have passed outside. Then again, time can move at the same speed as in the outer world. It is very unpredictable. Of course, from within, using the correct spell, the flow of time can be adjusted to match that of the world beyond. It seems that your new master, Hrothgar, was not concerned about that and allowed time to flow as it would.'

There was a long pause as I digested what had happened. Then my head was full of questions.

'Tom and Alice?' I asked. 'Where are they? Are they safe? And what happened to Tilda?'

Even before she replied I knew that I would not like what she told me. This had been a spook's house for many generations and had been left to Tom by his master John Gregory so that he could continue to serve the County. Tom believed in carrying out his duty. There was no way that he would have abandoned this house willingly.

'Alice was brave and powerful – perhaps one of the most powerful witches who has ever walked the earth,' Grimalkin told me. 'And she badly wanted to be reunited with her daughter. Despite Tom Ward doing all he could to dissuade her, Alice gathered her magic and attacked Circe in her lair. It is almost impossible for a witch to match the power of a goddess but Alice came very close to winning before being forced to retreat. Despite Tom Ward pleading with her not to repeat such a terrible risk, within one short month of her defeat, filled with a mother's fury, Alice attacked again. And this time Alice damaged Circe very badly. It wasn't a victory but it bought time – years when she and her family could live happily in relative safety . . .'

'So it was safe for Tilda. You were able to give her back to Alice?' I asked.

Grimalkin nodded and spoke again, showing those terrible teeth. 'Yes. Tom, Alice and Tilda lived together in happiness here for almost ten years. But it could not last. No matter how badly such a powerful goddess is damaged, unless totally destroyed she will regenerate and regain her strength. Circe sent her creatures against this Chipenden house. At first the attacks were minor and the boggart easily repelled them. Then one night the boggart was finally defeated. It lost its other eye and now is blind. And it took all of Alice's magic just to repel Circe. The danger continued to grow and once more I took Tilda to a place of safety.'

What place was safe from a goddess? How could you hide from such a powerful being? I didn't want to hear the end of Grimalkin's narrative – it could only end badly – but I forced myself to listen.

'One night, the inevitable happened. Circe attacked and won. Tom and Alice disappeared and have not been seen since. Tilda is safe for now but I do not know how much longer I will be able to protect her.'

Then an astonishing realization hit me.

'Tilda! I held her as a baby – it just seems a few months ago, but she'll be fourteen now!' I exclaimed.

'Yes, she is far beyond a baby now,' Grimalkin stated. 'She is clever, wilful and proud. And when she becomes a woman, Tilda might have magical power beyond even that of her mother – if she lives to maturity.'

'And Tom and Alice? Do you think they're dead?' I asked.

'That is very likely, but there is a small chance that Circe holds them prisoners somewhere and they still live. She may one day hope to use them both as a bargaining counter to snare their daughter in some way. Circe would do anything to drink the blood of Tilda.'

Then I suddenly felt ashamed. I had not enquired about the one person who'd been with me when I was taken. 'Spook Johnson?' I asked. 'What happened to him?'

Grimalkin frowned. 'Johnson is not the man he was. That broken leg left him with a bad limp and that has taken much of his confidence from him. He did spend quite some time with Tom and Alice searching for you, but when that came to nothing, deterred by them from trying to deal with the Pendle clans – although together they had cleared a clan of witches from a manor house in Billinge – he wandered the County dealing with witches wherever he could find them. At last, despite advice and finally pleas from Tom and Alice not to do so, Johnson made a foolish attempt to interfere with the Pendle clans. Alice begged me to intervene and, with great reluctance, I saved him from death and gained him his freedom. Now he is back at the millhouse dealing with the occasional water witch. But he is a shadow of his former self.'

I felt sorry for Johnson. He had been big and strong – a formidable fighter. He would find it hard to adjust to that change to his body and the limitations it would bring. Hrothgar had said that the damage to his body would make him a better person. But I knew Spook Johnson better than that, so I doubted it. As Grimalkin had said, his injury had affected him permanently, for the worse. That saddened me.

'Perhaps I should visit him,' I said, talking to myself more than Grimalkin.

'That would be foolish, child, because you are in grave danger. Circe never forgets. She will seek to pay you back for allying yourself with Tom Ward and Alice. In that underworld you were protected and invisible to her, but now she will know that you are back in this world and she will be searching for you. Go back to Hrothgar and accept the further training that he offers – that is the best advice I can offer. Will you heed my words?'

I nodded. What choice did I have?

'Farewell. I may visit you again soon. I have much to consider and must do what is for the best. I promised Alice that were she not able to do so, then I would make provision for Tilda . . .'

The glow faded and I was alone in the room.

Exhausted, I lay back on the bed, full of sadness for Tom and Alice, until eventually my eyelids became heavy and I slowly drifted off to sleep. —

I awoke as the grey dawn light slowly filtered into the room. Wasting no time, I went downstairs. As I opened the back door, I glanced at Tom Ward's staff leaning in the corner.

Without thinking, I picked it up and carried it away. As I crossed the garden, I heard the boggart whining somewhere off amongst the trees. It sounded like it was in distress. Was it wailing for the loss of its sight – or perhaps for the absence of Tom and Alice whom it had failed to protect?

Once clear of the garden I went a little out of my way to avoid the village of Chipenden. I didn't want another conversation with the nosy butcher.

Soon I was heading in the direction of the underworld. I would do as Grimalkin advised. After all, what chance did I have against Circe and her servants? I did feel a certain pang at not being able to visit Spook Johnson though. I wasn't sure how I could help him but I felt that I owed him something. After all, I'd been his apprentice and we'd shared lots of dangers together. Carrying Tom's staff made me feel like a spook's apprentice again.

I'd had no breakfast and by noon I was really hungry. I pulled out the last piece of bread and a morsel of cheese – all that remained of what Hrothgar had given me. The bread was almost stale but I devoured it anyway. As I ate, I kept walking – but more slowly than on my journey north.

It was late in the afternoon the following day when I finally reached the boundary of the underworld. I glanced across to Mother Martha's cottage and noted that the door was closed. So I walked on and passed between the invisible gate marked by the two tall sycamores. The daylight sky of grey cloud cover was immediately replaced by night and a cloudless sky devoid of stars yet glowing a baleful red.

I entered the trees with some trepidation. Hrothgar had promised me that the monstrous guardians would recognize me and not attack. I was very nervous, and with my heart hammering I advanced slowly and cautiously. All I could hear was the rhythmical sound of my boots and my own rapid breathing. Beneath the trees all else was silent, and if the tulpa beasts watched me, I saw no sign of them.

That had not been my only worry. Time itself was a concern. I might spend a little time here now then discover that again many years had passed outside – maybe everyone I'd ever known would be dead? It was a terrifying thought.

I crossed the bridge over the moat and, keeping to the path, walked through the sunken garden. The windows of the mansion were in darkness. I wondered if Hrothgar would be surprised to see me return so soon. At last I climbed the steps. As I got closer, I could see the abhuman still kneeling close to the front door of the house. But its original position had changed.

It was not facing towards the house. It was facing away from it and towards me.

As I approached, I was surprised by the fact that it lifted its head and stared directly at me. Then the creature clambered to its feet and took a step nearer. I felt threatened and took a step backwards, gripping Tom Ward's staff more tightly. But I would have little chance if it attacked. I remembered how easily it had dealt with the formidable Spook Johnson.

Then the creature spoke. 'My master waited for you but you stayed away too long. Now it is too late. Come with me and see what he bade me to show you . . .'

The abhuman walked to the front left corner of the house and I followed, puzzled at what he meant. I had been away no more than a few days. Unless the speed of time within the underworld had changed again? Maybe time was moving faster within this world?

We walked down the side of the mansion and onto a large lawn at the rear. My heart sank as I realized what was the object of our visit.

In the middle of the lawn was a grave with a headstone. The grave had the usual width but was almost twelve feet long and I knew before reading the inscription who was buried there.

Hrothgar was dead.

14

THE LEGACY

I read the carving on the tombstone. It was brief and to the point.

HERE LIETH HROTHGAR
MAY HE REST IN ETERNAL PEACE

'My master left you a letter,' the abhuman told me, then gestured that I should follow and turned on its heels before walking towards the front of the mansion. It seemed wrong to leave the grave so abruptly but I followed the tulpa anyway. Once inside, I noticed a change to the large hallway. Before there had been only five doors. Now there were seven. Had there been that number there all along but somehow I hadn't been able to see them? Had Hrothgar used magic to deceive me?

The creature opened one of the new doors on the far left and showed me into a large L-shaped room.

Clearly this had been a study for Hrothgar. There was a big leather-topped desk and a comfortable chair positioned before it. On the floor, at the side of the desk, was a large wooden chest. Then there was a long table with three chairs facing another three across its width. The walls of the study were lined with books, the shelves extending upwards to the high ceiling, with ladders positioned at intervals along the walls. This was more of a library than a study: it contained an extensive stock of books to rival that at Tom Ward's Chipenden house.

There was a white envelope on the desk, one word written upon it.

WULF

'I will leave you alone so that you may read my master's wishes in private,' said the abhuman. Then the creature left the room.

Leaning Tom's staff against the wall, I sat down at the desk, carefully opened the envelope, took out the letter and unfolded it. Then I began to read.

Dear Wulf,
I had hoped to have time to continue your training but it seems that is not to be. As I write this, my last letter, my heart is rapidly failing. I am weak and breathless and soon I will die. It will be difficult but, by using

the resources of my library, it may be possible for you to learn all that you need to know and further develop your abilities. I hope you will try your best to do so.

To you I leave all my possessions: everything within the boundaries of the underworld that I have created. I also leave to you the gatekeeper's cottage. By now all my servants but one have ceased to exist. The final tulpa, soon after giving you this letter, will also pass away.

You will have to buy your own food from the local village which is called King's Moss. There is coin in the chest that should last you for many years. Remember, each time you venture forth, it is vital that you use the cottage as a way station. You may be followed or watched and that is the method which has been used successfully for many years to conceal the presence of this underworld.

All that was mine now belongs to you. Keep it safe and use it well.

Despite any difficulties that you may encounter, please exercise your abilities to make this world a better place for all.

My very best wishes for the future,
Hrothgar

I left the letter on the desk and knelt beside the wooden chest. It wasn't locked and I raised the lid to see what it contained. There were small compartments each containing different denominations of coin. There was gold, silver and copper. If I stayed here, I certainly would not go hungry.

That was if I chose to stay . . .

The death of Hrothgar changed things significantly. I felt sad, with a great sense of loss. After our initial terrifying meeting, I had gradually come to trust and respect him. He had saved my life by helping me to overcome that inner self that would have destroyed me. I had come here in the confidence that he would continue my training and make me good at my craft. Now that wasn't to be. But this was still a place of refuge and I certainly paid heed to Grimalkin's warning. However, the thought of being alone here was daunting.

I closed the lid of the chest and walked deeper into the library until I reached the far wall. Then I turned right and saw a door which had been out of sight round the corner. I opened it and found myself in a long narrow passageway with the usual high ceiling typical of the house. There were no windows but there were small torches in brackets attached to the walls and, as I entered, they immediately flared up and lit the corridor. There was only one door and it was right at the end, so I slowly walked towards it.

One thing was very clear. This mansion was certainly far larger on the inside than it appeared from the outside. This and the flickering torches were more of Hrothgar's magic. This was an underworld and the physical laws of the outer world did not apply here. I paused outside the door at the end of the long passageway.

It was painted black and was the usual shape, very high and designed to accommodate Hrothgar.

Then I noticed something very unusual. The door had no lock – not even a handle.

I pressed my hand against it but the door did not yield. I was puzzled. Hrothgar had left this house to me. All within this underworld was mine. Surely this was part of my legacy, so why could I not enter the room beyond this door?

Without a lock or a handle, I was not sure what could be done to open it but I concentrated, counted down from five to zero and summoned Saint Quentin.

His long bony hand came over my shoulder, but this time he wasn't clutching a key. The saint placed his palm against the door. I could hear faint sounds as if something was whirring and clicking within it. Was there some kind of inner mechanism that kept the door locked?

Saint Quentin persisted for almost five minutes. He tried hard, but the tulpa failed and eventually faded away. I had not been able to get the door open, so my curiosity was high.

What could be concealed behind it?

Then a shiver of fear ran down my spine. Underworlds were a bridge between the human world and Hell. Was this an actual doorway to the dark?

I put my ear against the door and heard faint sounds from beyond it – a rhythmical whispering. I pressed my head closer to the door which was as cold as ice, but I could make no sense of what was being said. The noise was faint and indistinct but I could make out similarities in the sounds.

The same words were being repeated over and over again as if demons were praying to a greater beast of the dark.

I stepped back and was gripped by fear again. There was something immensely powerful beyond that door. I still wanted to see what lay behind it, but I sensed danger. Despite my intense curiosity, I knew what I must do. I walked away.

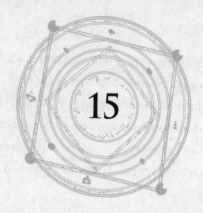

15

YOUR MOTHER'S DAUGHTER

Early the following evening, carrying the empty hessian sack, I passed between the two tall sycamores and left the underworld.

I wondered how much time had elapsed here during my stay in the underworld of just one night. There were fresh green leaves on the trees and it still seemed like early summer but for all I knew years might have passed by.

I walked towards the cottage and, taking the key from my breeches pocket, unlocked the front door and entered. It was gloomy inside and the air was damp. I half expected to find the clothes of Mother Martha on the floor where they had fallen as she ceased to exist. But there was nothing and I realized that Hrothgar would have summoned her into the underworld before he died. He would have done that so that no suspicious traces of her could be found by others.

Mother Martha had tidied the cottage thoroughly before she left. In the kitchen, the plates had been washed and stacked in cupboards and the knives and forks were in the cutlery drawer. Not one thing was out of place in any of the rooms that I entered. The giant would have instructed her to do that. I wondered if she'd had an inkling that she wouldn't be returning. I hoped that wasn't the case and she'd never even suspected what she really was.

I found a letter in the parlour. It was pinned to the window ledge by the blade of a small dagger. I opened it and began to read. It was short and to the point:

> *Wait by the sycamores just after dark.*
> *I need to speak to you urgently.*
> Grimalkin

I shivered. What did she want to say to me now? I had a feeling that it wouldn't be anything good. But it was a good couple of hours before dark so I'd plenty of time to get my shopping done.

I left the cottage, locking the door behind me, and walked down the hill towards the village, which lay only a couple of miles from Hrothgar's house and on the route north towards Chipenden. It proved to be small with just a single narrow cobbled street and three shops – a baker, a butcher and a grocery store. I bought a loaf of bread without trouble because the shop was full and the proprietor was too busy to give me more than a second glance. But as soon as I walked into the butcher's and saw that I was the only customer, I knew I had a problem. The way he glared at me and looked me up and down reminded me of the butcher at Chipenden, but although this man was as tall, probably about six feet in height, he had a shiny bald head.

'And what can I do for *you*, young man?' he demanded.

'I'd like six pork sausages, and two pounds of minced beef, and a small chicken please,' I replied.

He nodded and cut the six sausages from a larger string of sausages before weighing the mince, choosing a small chicken and wrapping everything in greased paper.

'New to the area, are you? Can't remember seeing your face before . . .'

'I'm staying at Mother Martha's cottage for a while.'

'Are you now? But she was in recently – earlier this week – and she said she was going away to stay with a relative who'd been taken ill. That's what she told me,' he said with a frown.

I'd wondered how long it was since the butcher had last seen her. And now I knew. For no matter the difference whilst I'd been away in Chipenden, time was now passing at the same rate on both sides of the gate to the underworld.

'That's right,' I replied. 'I'm her nephew and she sent me back to look after the cottage while she's away and do a few repairs that are long overdue. So that means I'll be here for some time.'

I could feel the butcher's eyes following me as I walked out of his shop. I sensed that he wasn't quite convinced by my story but I shrugged and went into the grocer's. It was even busier than the baker's and I had to queue out in the street just to get into the shop. The grocer was run off his feet dashing back and forth to fill each order, so thankfully there was no time for conversation with him at all. But lots of eyes were on me. Everybody knew everybody else and I was a stranger. People were naturally curious.

Back at Mother Martha's cottage I waited for dark. I watched through the windows until the light began to fail and then, certain that I hadn't been followed, I left with my sack of food and headed directly towards the two sycamores to wait for Grimalkin.

I didn't have long to wait. A faint glow appeared in the distance and then I could see Grimalkin walking towards me. But she wasn't alone.

There was a young girl carrying a large leather bag walking at her side.

'This is Tilda, the daughter of Tom Ward and Alice Deane. I believe you have met her before,' Grimalkin said, a faint smile on her face.

I stared at Tilda, not knowing what to say. I could clearly see her resemblance to Alice. She had her mother's dark hair and pretty face with high-boned cheeks and vivacious eyes. She held herself very erect and was as tall as I was.

'I last saw you when you were just a baby,' I blurted out.

Tilda nodded but didn't smile. She looked neither happy nor friendly. When she spoke, it was to address Grimalkin, not me.

'Must I do this?' she demanded haughtily.

'You must, child, but I have yet to explain to Wulf what I require. Wulf, I want you to ask your master to give Tilda refuge in his underworld. I can no longer keep her safe.'

Before I could reply, Tilda spoke again. 'Grimalkin, why do we always need to hide? Together we could destroy Circe. It need not be too difficult.'

Grimalkin smiled and showed her pointy teeth. 'You are indeed your mother's daughter, Tilda, but I still advise extreme caution. You need to develop your magic. When you are older, we may indeed combine our strength and move against her but that time has not yet come.'

'But my mother and father may still be alive, suffering at the hands of that evil goddess. How can we allow that to continue?'

'Because we must, child. To attack now might result in our destruction – and how would that help your parents?'

Tilda didn't reply but just bowed her head and gazed at the ground.

'Will you do as I ask, Wulf?' Grimalkin demanded.

I looked at the scary glowing witch assassin with blades attached to the shoulder straps that crossed her body and the necklace of thumb-bones around her neck. I wondered what she would do if I refused.

'Yes,' I replied.

'Good. You will not regret it.'

'But there's something that you should know,' I protested. 'Hrothgar is dead, and now I'll have to train myself using his library as best I can. He left the underworld and all it contains to me but I'm not sure that I can defend it from intruders.'

'I am sorry to hear that but you needn't worry on that score. Any underworld has natural defences, so for now you are hidden and safe. You and Tilda will be good company for each other. And this girl has magic enough of her own to stabilize the passage of time within and match it to the movement of time here.'

Tilda glared at me, her eyes flashing angrily. No doubt she was annoyed by the suggestion that we would be 'good company'.

'I will speak to you both again when it becomes necessary – here, where we are standing now,' said the witch assassin. Grimalkin turned to Tilda and placed her left hand on her shoulder. The expression on her face changed. Gone was the harsh predatory glare of the killer witch assassin. There was something much softer there – almost a look that a mother might give a daughter.

It only lasted one brief moment. Then Grimalkin faded away into nothingness and I was left alone with Tilda. I smiled at her, hoisted the sack over my right shoulder and walked towards the invisible gate. In return she scowled at me, but at least she followed, carrying her bag.

'What's in the sack?' she asked me.

'Food that I bought in the village – bread, sausages, minced meat, chicken, eggs, potatoes and vegetables.'

'Are you a good cook?'

I shrugged. 'I do my best. I can fry things. I'll get better.'

'In that case I'd better cook tonight.'

I didn't argue. After cooking for Spook Johnson, I could just about manage to do a good bacon, eggs and sausages, but apart from that limited skill with a frying pan I was probably the worst cook in the world.

'What's in *your* bag?' I asked.

'All the clothes I own and a few things that I value.'

She didn't explain what they were and I considered it rude to ask.

We passed through the gate and suddenly the sky was again a baleful red. As we trudged on through the trees, I pointed upwards. 'This isn't the most cheerful of places,' I said.

'I've spent time in far worse locations. Circe's servants were constantly at our heels and Grimalkin had to keep finding new hiding places for me. I even spent a short time in the dark itself.'

I didn't reply but I didn't like the sound of that. The dark was the name that witches used for Hell. This pretty girl walking beside me was a young witch who had even spent time in the infernal region. Hell was something that I had always feared – the home of demons and of evil goddesses such as Circe. I had entered Circe's terrifying underworld and that was as close to Hell as I ever wanted to get. It made me uneasy to learn that Tilda had taken refuge in the darkness and, guided by Grimalkin, had used it in order to survive.

'Oh! I like that!' Tilda cried out suddenly, pointing towards the house. 'It's very grand. How many rooms does it have?'

'Lots. You can have your pick.'

As we walked up the steps towards the house, Tilda started to smile. When we entered by the front door, she was grinning from ear to ear. 'I love this!' she exclaimed. 'I like the high roof, the tall door and the high windows above the lower ones. It's very unusual.'

'It had to be like that,' I explained, 'because Hrothgar, the owner, was a giant about eleven feet tall. But that's what killed him. He couldn't stop growing and eventually his heart wasn't strong enough to maintain his circulation.'

'That's sad,' said Tilda. 'Did he live a long life? How old was he?'

I shrugged. 'I don't know. It was one of the things I meant to ask him but never got around to it. Maybe now I'll never know.'

'Have you moved into his bedroom?' Tilda asked. 'After all, you're the master here now and everything belongs to you, doesn't it?'

I shook my head. 'I've only been inside it once, just to take a quick look. I sleep in the room that he chose for me. I wouldn't like to take his room because I don't think I'd be comfortable sleeping there. I'll probably just stay where I am.'

'Shall we look at it now?' she asked.

'Should I show you the rest of the house first?' I asked.

I did that and Tilda liked everything that I showed her including Hrothgar's study with its large library. As we walked down the corridor, Tilda stopped suddenly by the big black door at the end of the passageway, as if she could sense the power emanating from it. I'd already been back to it and tried again to open it since my first attempt. But I'd failed once more. Now the same thing happened to Tilda and I saw the anger and frustration in her face.

'Have you ever tried to open this door?' she asked.

I nodded. 'I tried and failed. I'm curious about what's beyond it but there's something scary about it.'

Tilda frowned and nodded. 'You're right. There's formidable magic keeping it closed and I sense a mysterious power beyond it. For now, it's best to leave it alone but one day we should open it. I'm just as curious as you are.'

Finally, I brought her to the door of Hrothgar's room and opened it for her, letting her walk inside before me.

The room was big but had little furniture. There was a small table with a couple of books on it, a chair and, of course, the bed which was very unusual. It had the normal breadth of a single bed but was twice as long.

'Why's the bed so long and narrow?' she asked.

'It's just right for him. As I told you, he was tall but thin.'

She nodded. 'It's good to have a wide bed so that you've plenty of room, so I don't know why he didn't have it made that way. But it'll do nicely for me. I think I'll sleep here if you don't mind,' she said, pulling the blanket back to examine the sheets. 'The bed seems to have been changed so this'll do fine. Did he have servants to do that for him?'

'Yes, but they were all tulpas. You do know what tulpas are?'

For a moment Tilda looked annoyed. 'Of course I do. I'm my mother's daughter, don't forget! She taught me a lot and she knew quite a bit about tulpas herself.'

In that flash of anger, I really could see her resemblance to Alice. A fierce light glared from Tilda's eyes and she stiffened her back and held herself in a way that projected every inch of her height.

'Well, now Hrothgar's dead his tulpas no longer exist. From now on, we'll have to change our own sheets,' I told her.

'Yes, and do our own cooking, Wulf. So let's make a start. I'm really hungry. Let's go back to the kitchen!'

As we turned to leave, I looked at Hrothgar's bed. I couldn't imagine sleeping there. He might have died in that bed.

'Don't you mind sleeping in a dead man's bed?' I blurted out.

Tilda shook her head. 'Can't throw a good bed out just because someone's died in it. That would be such a waste. No, this couldn't be better! I feel that he slept well in this long bed and had good dreams. I expect I'll do the same.'

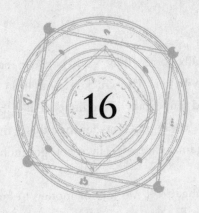

16

A Splinter of Your Soul

I led the way to the kitchen. Once there, Tilda wasted no time in raiding my sack of food and organizing things, quickly making it clear that I was to play my part in preparing the meal.

'Wulf, you can peel the potatoes and slice the carrots and I'll deal with the chicken. Did you buy any herbs?'

I shook my head. 'I wouldn't know what to ask for . . .'

'Then your education will start tomorrow!' Tilda said with a smile and, undaunted, she started to open cupboard doors until she found what she needed – a few small bunches of dried herbs hanging from hooks.

It was quite some time before the meal was ready and the aromas from the cooking were driving me to distraction but, at last, we sat down together and began to eat. It was delicious.

'This is really good, Tilda,' I said between mouthfuls.

'I can do better. The chicken is a little overcooked and I lacked important ingredients. I like braising and casseroles – they're much tastier than this. I think we'll go shopping again tomorrow. Have you got money for more food?'

'Yes, Hrothgar left me lots of money to buy food, but that's not the problem. Going down to the village too often might draw attention to us. There are two Quisitors operating in the County and on the lookout for witches and spooks. At the moment they aren't venturing out much, but if any of the villagers get suspicious, they might report us. The butcher was nosy and I had to concoct a story saying that the lady who owned the cottage had asked me to carry out repairs whilst she was away. I'm not really sure that he believed me. He seemed suspicious. How will I explain you?'

'Oh, just say that I'm your sister. Just leave the butcher to me. He'll pose no problem, I can promise you that.'

I shrugged. I could see that once Tilda made up her mind to do something, she did it, so I saved my breath and we continued eating. At last our plates were clean. I was full and couldn't have eaten another mouthful.

'Look, Tilda, that was a really nice meal. Thanks for cooking it. I know you don't really want to be here and I'll be honest. I can tell you don't like me much and, at first, I thought you were going to be difficult and unpleasant. But I was wrong and I apologize for that.'

She gave a long sigh. 'You're quite right. I don't want to be here but I've just got to make the best of it, haven't I? I usually try to be nice to people even if I don't like them much because manners cost nothing. But I do intend to be really difficult and really unpleasant when I finally meet up with Circe. And as for not liking you, we'll have to wait and see. I've not made my mind up about you yet, but at least you're honest and not afraid to tell me how you feel. So that's a good start. Now I'm tired so I'm off to bed. As I did most of the cooking, would you mind washing up the pots and pans?'

'Of course,' I said. 'That's only fair.'

'Well, tomorrow we'll take a proper look at that library and we'll make a start on your training.'

'You're going to help me?'

'Why not – it'll keep boredom at bay. My mother once watched someone make a tulpa and I remember what she told me. So I just might be able to help.'

After washing and drying the pots and pans, I went to bed, slept well and didn't dream. In an underworld that was in perpetual night with a red sky devoid of stars, there was no way to mark the passage of time. But I estimated that I could have slept seven or eight hours.

I was really hungry and made straight for the kitchen. When I walked in, Tilda was already there, frying eggs.

'Eggs on toast enough for you?' she asked. 'Best to have a light breakfast because we need our minds sharp. We've lots of information to sort through.'

'Yes please!' I said. But the truth was that I'd have preferred something more substantial.

As we ate, we talked. Tilda certainly liked to chat and never ran out of things to say. Wasting no time, she started telling me what she knew about tulpas.

'I mentioned yesterday that my mother watched a tulpa being made. Well, actually there were two but the second one is more interesting. It was a tulpa that actually believed it was a spook called Bill Arkwright—'

'I read a book written by Bill Arkwright!' I exclaimed. 'He was an expert on water witches but died in Greece, I believe.'

'He was, Wulf, I know all about him, but don't interrupt me when I'm speaking. It's rude.'

'Sorry,' I said, chastened by her rebuke.

Tilda nodded and gave me a little smile and then continued with her tale. 'Well, Bill had helped to train my father and spent six months toughening him up, but he was supposed to have been killed overseas – in a country called Greece, as you said.

'Then years later he turned up at the mill near the canal – the place he used to work from. My father totally believed that he was talking to Spook Arkwright. But eventually the creature became confused and said it couldn't remember certain things and became unsure about its own identity. Finally, my father guessed the truth and named it – telling it that it was indeed a tulpa. Just saying that to its face was enough to destroy it. Before it died it said something that my father never forgot.

'It cried out, "Even a dog has more soul than me. I'm a thing without a soul. From nothing I came and to nothing I will return!" And within moments it disintegrated and all that remained was its clothes and a faint stench of rot. Don't you think that's terrible?'

'Yes, that's what puts me off most about creating such creatures,' I replied. 'They don't ask to be created, and eventually they might be confronted with what they truly are. That really is horrible.'

'I agree, Wulf. Put like that it certainly is, but if they never find out they could have a happy existence. And isn't it the same for us too? We didn't ask to be born either, did we? And we don't always know who we are or what we are.'

Then I had a puzzling thought. 'If your mother knew that Arkwright was a tulpa, why didn't she tell your father?'

Tilda shrugged and shook her head. 'My mother wasn't at his side when he met the tulpa so she couldn't tell him that. It's one of the things they didn't like to talk about. An evil mage called Lukrasta created the tulpa and somehow my mother was in his power. But it all turned out all right in the end. She killed Lukrasta. Chopped his head off with a sword, I believe. But, as I said, they wouldn't talk about it much and I certainly don't know the details of what happened. But I do know that my father was certainly with her on that occasion. So why did he leave my mother to kill the mage? Parents! They certainly like to keep their secrets. Even Grimalkin wouldn't tell me the full story.'

I stared at her as she sat there calmly eating her last mouthful of toast. It was an astonishing story. Alice was a witch, but she was also nice and kind and had been a good mother to Tilda. I couldn't imagine her using a sword like that . . .

'Well,' said Tilda, 'you can wash up later. Take me to the library so that we can make a start.'

Once in there Tilda immediately took control. The first thing she did was light the candles on the large table using her magic. There were five of them and one glance from Tilda and they immediately flickered to life.

Then she noticed the staff that I'd left leaning against the wall. 'That's one of my father's staffs, isn't it?' she asked.

'Yes, I brought it with me when I visited the Chipenden house recently. I only borrowed it,' I said, by way of apology lest she think I'd stolen it.

'I hate those staffs! Nasty things they are, made of rowan wood. Can't bear to touch it!'

I said nothing. Like her mother, Tilda was clearly a witch. No wonder she didn't like that staff, even though it was her father's.

'What's in that big chest?' she asked next.

'That's where Hrothgar kept his money. There's lots of it,' I replied, walking over and throwing back the lid.

'Well, we certainly aren't going to go hungry,' Tilda said with a smile. 'But now we need pens and paper so that we can make notes. There could be some in one of the drawers,' she said, nodding in the direction of the big desk, clearly indicating that I should search for what we needed.

I walked over to the leather-topped desk and began opening the drawers one at a time. There were six in all, but I found paper, pens and a bottle of ink in the third one that I tried.

'Bring everything across to the big table,' Tilda said.

I did as she said and we sat down opposite each other.

'Right,' she said. 'Before we start to read, show me what you can do. I want to see one of your tulpas.'

'I've not got very far . . .'

'Look, Wulf, don't make excuses. Just show me and let me be the judge of what you achieve. If you lacked talent, Hrothgar wouldn't have taken you on as his apprentice, would he? He certainly wouldn't have left you his house and all his possessions. So please have a little faith in yourself.'

I nodded, closed my eyes and started to concentrate. I knew I could express a tulpa briefly, so I attempted to manifest Raphael, who'd saved me from the monster under my bed. It proved harder than usual – probably because I was distracted by the presence of Tilda – but I persevered.

Finally I fell back on my old method of summoning a saint using prayer. But I did it silently.

'Raphael! I beseech thee. Please hear me. Be at my side!'

I sensed the approach of the tulpa whilst I repeated the prayer. I also finally used the deep concentration technique that Hrothgar had taught me, by counting down from five to zero.

There was a flutter in the air to my right, a movement over the table not too far from my right shoulder, a suggestion of white wings. Then Raphael manifested fully. It lasted for hardly more than a few seconds but he was there, solid and vividly colourful, floating high above the table.

With his huge white wings unfurled, Raphael wore a bright blue robe and black leather belt and boots, his long hair gleaming like gold. He held his sword high, gripping it with both hands as if prepared to deliver a killing stroke. He stared down at me and, as our eyes met, he vanished.

'Well, Wulf, I knew you could do it and that proves it. But how can you make a tulpa stick around longer?' Tilda asked.

'That skill could take years to develop – that's what I hope to learn from the books in this library,' I said, gesturing at the shelves. 'Hrothgar once told me I could have a tulpa as a companion but it would mean using blood, bone and dust. That kind of tulpa is called a gristle, but I don't want to make one and have tulpa servants like he did. The other kind is called wraiths, but they are just formed out of thin air using imagination. It's harder to make them last. But that's the type I'm going to make.'

'My mother said that the evil mage created the tulpa of Bill Arkwright using blood and dust, so he must have been a gristle. I think you're doing the right thing to make a wraith but I'm sure you wouldn't want someone like the creature with wings and a sword. Who *was* that?'

'It was Saint Raphael, who some think was an archangel. Before I learned what I was, I used to pray to saints and some of them manifested and helped me . . .'

I went on to explain how I had been in peril of the monster under my bed, my Bane, and how Raphael had cut its hand off and plunged his sword into its lair.

'I think my parents once had a scary confrontation with a creature called the "Bane",' said Tilda. 'It was trapped behind a silver gate, confined to a labyrinth under Priestown Cathedral. It's another thing they wouldn't talk about much – so I never got the full story. But that's an interesting word, "bane". It means something poisonous or dangerous –

something that can cause death. Did you know that there's a poisonous plant called aconite? But most people know it by another name – *wolfsbane*! A long time ago it was used to poison wolves.'

'Nice to know that my name's linked to a poison!' I said jokingly.

Tilda grinned back at me and then became more serious. 'I thought *I'd* been having some scary times,' she said, 'but that must be as bad as it can get. Despite him saving you, Raphael wouldn't be a very suitable companion, would he? I mean, imagine the reaction if you walked into a town or village with him!' She laughed. 'Besides, a tulpa believes it is what you make it to be. He would really think he was a saint. No, you need something else. I'll think about it and get back to you when I've decided what's best.'

Tilda was nice but she was more than a little bossy. I would make my own mind up. I didn't think I'd ever want even a temporary tulpa companion anyway – something that could just stick around for a short while was enough for me. But I smiled at Tilda and then decided to take the lead for once.

'Right!' I said. 'Let's get started. We could begin by searching through a few titles and then choosing to read the most likely ones to be helpful. Then we could make notes, summarizing what we learn.'

Tilda's mouth opened and closed again and she looked surprised at my taking the initiative, but she quickly took over again. 'You take that wall of shelves and I'll take this one. Let's allow about ten minutes or so to make our first selection.'

I nodded and we began. I started by looking at the books on the shelves within easy reach but then, on impulse, I climbed one of the ladders and searched a shelf right at the very top of the library.

Immediately, a book bound in soft brown calfskin caught my eye.

The Difficulty in Choosing a Bound Tulpa by K. Hrothgar

I remembered Hrothgar instructing me about a bound tulpa. One thing appealed to me about such a creature. He'd said that it would not be destroyed by the horror of finally learning exactly what its true nature was. It seemed to me that a tulpa that could come to terms with that was preferable to something that always had to be shielded from the truth.

Curiously, I eased the book from its position on the shelf and carefully descended the ladder, clutching it in my left hand.

Tilda was already seated at the table, a book open before her. She'd said we'd have ten minutes to choose but it had taken me much less than that and Tilda had been even faster.

The book I had chosen was very slim and was in the neat handwriting of Hrothgar. I began to read and soon it became clear that he was discussing a companion similar to what Tilda and I had talked about earlier. It was a companion closely bound to its creator – hence the title of the book.

Bound tulpas can be either gristles or wraiths - both types are suitable but I must make it clear that I do indeed regret never having created a bound tulpa. By desisting I have deprived myself of one of the most satisfactory experiences open to a tulpar. But I could never bring myself to create such an entity. I lacked the courage to divide my soul. Thus, the tulpas that I created have all been human or half-human servants, not truly bound, and with that came a necessary distance. But who knows? It may well be an option that I take up in the remote future.

There was no date in the book so I had no idea how long ago those words had been written. Had he ever gone on to create such a bound tulpa?

I read on, quickly skimming through much of what Hrothgar had written. He seemed to be agonizing over the problem; he was pleased to have made the decision not to have created a bound tulpa at that point, and yet worrying about what he might have missed.

I decided to make short summaries of the points that Hrothgar made. Rather than using the paper on the table I pulled out my notebook. I opened it and then hesitated.

'That's a nice notebook,' Tilda commented. 'What's the problem? You don't look happy.'

'It's what your father gave me and I'm supposed to use it to make notes about the things I learn as a spook's apprentice. But this is different. It's information for somebody training to be a tulpar like Hrothgar. I don't want to get the two sets of notes mixed up.'

'The answer is simple!' Tilda explained with a grin. 'Make it into a flip-book. Turn the notebook upside down, then start writing from the back page towards the front. That will keep the notes separate.'

'Great idea!' I said, returning her smile. Then I did as she'd advised. After all, I was now two things: a spook's apprentice and a trainee tulpar.

In the book there was a short section on what type of tulpa was best suited to be bound to a human master. Warrior human tulpas seemed to be Hrothgar's preferred option but I noted that other types of creatures, including dogs and bats, had been used by other tulpars. Again, that felt to me uncomfortably close to the way that some witches used familiars.

The book was very short, and in my opinion was mostly nothing more than a confession of how torn he had been between creating and not creating such a being. Reading between the lines, I felt that the truth was that he regretted it very much. It did not explain how to create such a special tulpa but it did end with the following short paragraph:

A bound tulpa is more than a mere companion; it is an extension of its creator's soul. But it brings risks as well as benefits. If a bound tulpa is hurt by a hostile force, then its creator is also injured. If the tulpa is slain, its creator may also die.

But despite the risks, there are great benefits to be had. A bound tulpa uses a splinter of its creator's soul and he can look out through its eyes and sense everything that it does.

That was enough to give anyone pause for thought. A splinter of your soul was transferred to the tulpa! Then I suddenly remembered how I'd looked through the eyes of Raphael. It hadn't lasted long but it had seemed real enough. Had I started to make a bound tulpa without realizing it? It seemed unlikely that such a thing would just happen by chance – especially for such a novice tulpar as myself – so I dismissed it from my mind. I glanced across to see that Tilda was scribbling furiously, making a list. She saw me watching her, smiled and showed me the cover of the book she was making notes from.

I read the title.

How to Prolong the Existence of a Tulpa

I might have known it! Tilda had found the exact
information that we'd been searching for . . .

17

CLOSE YOUR ARROGANT MOUTH!

'Shall we swap books for a while?' Tilda asked.

I nodded and passed mine across to her. When she handed me her book, I reached across for her notes but she shook her head and pulled the paper out of reach.

'Better to read it yourself first!' she told me. 'As I said, you might spot something that I missed.'

It didn't take me long to read that slim volume. It repeated much of what Hrothgar had already taught me verbally, explaining how with focus and concentration upon an image within the mind, a wraith could eventually take on solid form in the outer world. It also detailed how to make a tulpa persist – how to make it a permanent creature that, like the abhuman he had taken for his servant, only disappeared when you died.

But to do that required the residue of desiccated plants, dust and ground bones mixed with cartilage and the fresh warm blood of an animal. It required the making of a gristle. I decided that I would never do that. Again, it reminded me too much of dark magic of the worst possible kind. No, my first tulpa would persist only for the time I needed it to accompany me and perform a task that I set before it. I would just use imagination to create it and summon it from pure air. And I would also make it persist by the exercise of my imagination. Surely, with lots of practice that would become possible and, in time, much easier?

As I closed the book, Tilda pushed her notes towards me. I read them quickly. 'You've missed nothing,' I told her with a smile.

'Good!' she said. 'Now let's take a break and go down into the village to buy the things I need for cooking. We can talk about this,' she said, nodding towards the two books, 'as we walk.'

Hrothgar had emphatically warned me to call in at the cottage after leaving the underworld and to wait there for a while to be sure nobody else was in the vicinity.

Now, stupidly, I broke that rule. One reason was because I was with Tilda and she was impatient to get down to the village. The second was because it was raining really hard. We emerged from the unchanging red sky of the underworld into a torrential downpour with low dark grey clouds blustering in from the west.

I could pull my hood up but Tilda was dressed in just a shirt, blouse and short leather jerkin with no protection at all for her head. I suggested that we go back to get her something more suitable to wear but she wouldn't hear of it. Walking fast because of the pouring rain, we exchanged few words and arrived at the village shops soaked to the skin, looking like two drowned rats.

I was also keen to get back as quickly as possible. I didn't know how much risk was involved but I feared that because we were out of the underworld, Circe might be able to detect and find us. Her servants might be racing towards us already. And who knew what terrible beasts they might prove to be?

Once again, it was the butcher who had all the questions.

'Well, who's the young lady?' he asked, with a sardonic grin. 'Looks to me like she comes from a place where it never rains!'

I looked at Tilda and saw her through the butcher's eyes. Her clothes were saturated and her black hair was plastered to her scalp with rain, rivulets of which were running down her forehead and dripping from her nose and chin.

'This is my sister,' I lied to the butcher. 'She's staying at the cottage with me. Whilst I do the repairs, she's going to clean it thoroughly from top to bottom.'

The butcher frowned at me. 'Mother Martha is extremely house-proud. You could eat your dinner off her kitchen floor. There'll be no cleaning needs doing there. In fact, she'd be very angry indeed if you even *hinted* that any cleaning was necessary!'

I wasn't sure what reply to make but Tilda answered for me. 'Why don't you close your arrogant mouth and do your job!' she snapped.

I cringed at Tilda's words and glanced behind us, relieved that there was nobody else in the shop to hear that. The butcher's face reddened and he opened his mouth to make an angry retort, and no doubt to demand that we leave his shop immediately.

Then something happened that made me gasp. Suddenly the air became incredibly cold and I began to shiver, my heart thumping in my chest. But if I was badly affected it was far worse for the butcher who now seemed to be having trouble getting his words out. The expression in his eyes suggested that he was in pain. His mouth kept opening and closing, then he staggered backwards and almost fell.

I looked at Tilda again. Her expression was one of intense concentration and she was staring hard at the butcher. My heart sank. I knew that she was using Devil magic.

'Don't worry, because you'll feel a lot better in a few moments,' Tilda told him. 'Just as soon as you've served us with what we need. You could start with half a dozen of your best-quality lamb chops!'

The butcher completed our order, but didn't speak again even after Tilda paid him. He simply stared ahead, a dazed expression on his face.

Once out of the shop I turned on Tilda angrily. 'Why did you speak to him like that?' I demanded. 'The last thing we need is to draw attention to ourselves.'

'You're worrying for nothing, Wulf. A little magic can prove quite useful. When he's himself again he won't remember a single word that I said. He needed putting in his place.'

'Using magic in public like that isn't wise,' I told her. 'If anyone were to notice—'

'Leave the wisdom to me!' she retorted angrily. 'I've got more of it in my little finger than you have in your fat head!'

'You think so?' I responded angrily. 'Your mother would never have done something stupid like that!'

Instantly, as I blurted out those words, I regretted it. It had been very cruel of me to say that about Alice under the circumstances. When I glanced at Tilda she had her head down and I saw a tear trickle down her cheek.

'I'm sorry. I didn't mean to say that,' I told her.

She didn't reply. I glanced over my shoulder and saw a small, stout, grey-haired woman standing in the doorway of the butcher's shop. She wore a bloodied apron and was staring towards us angrily. Was that the butcher's wife? If she'd been in the back room, she might have overheard what had happened and she would have felt the strange coldness of the air. It made me very uneasy.

Our visits to the other shops went smoothly and soon we were climbing the hill back up to Hrothgar's house. I was carrying the sack of food as usual. But all the way back we walked in silence, which was partly a result of my anger at Tilda because of the way she'd behaved in the butcher's shop. Also, though, I was thinking hard about the first tulpa that I intended to create.

Tilda truly was an excellent cook and after a delicious lunch I'd washed the dishes and we were seated at the table again. She never mentioned what I'd said about Alice and seemed to have put it behind her. That was good. Some people nursed grievances and I was glad that Tilda wasn't like that.

Soon we'd skimmed through three more books each and made useful notes. It was then that Tilda leaned back in her chair and stared at me hard.

'The sooner you get started the better,' she told me. 'First you have to decide what your tulpa will be.'

'Well, I know that but I certainly don't want it to be like a person,' I replied. 'And I don't want to create something that one day might realize that it's a thing without a soul and die at that moment – like the tulpa that thought it was Spook Arkwright.' It seemed wrong to create something that appeared human, but wasn't, and couldn't know exactly what it was.

'So it needs to be some kind of creature then. To start with, perhaps something quite small that could even fit into your pocket? Maybe a kitten like the one Hrothgar created for you? Kittens have claws too. Cats certainly know how to defend themselves.'

'I've been thinking along the lines of something that can fly . . .'

'That's a great idea!' she said enthusiastically. 'Maybe a hawk of some kind – a hen harrier or a falcon?'

'I think it would be even better if it were something that doesn't already exist in the world. Something totally new that I create from my imagination. I'd also eventually like it to be a bound tulpa too, that will know exactly what its true nature is. Yes! It must be bound to me with a splinter of my soul, but definitely a wraith. I don't want to make a gristle – I don't even like the sound of the name.'

'A bound tulpa! That's ambitious for a first attempt,' she said. 'What would it look like?'

I'd already thought about it and made up my mind so the answer came to my lips very quickly. 'It would be a small furry creature with wings, but fierce, strong and able to defend itself – a sort of sky wolf.'

I blow out the candles and draw the curtain across the door so that the room is very dark. Then I find my way to the table and sit with my hands joined as if in prayer. While praying was not Hrothgar's method, I remember how he had once told me that if it made me feel comfortable then it could do no harm.

I concentrate and try to create the sky wolf. Time passes. Minutes become hours. I try everything that Hrothgar taught me. I lose track of the times that I count down from five to zero. Each time the explosion of my breath and will becomes more desperate. Eventually, I am rewarded by a tiny speck of light in the darkness. It's like a small glowing insect that flutters in the air close to my head. It is too small to make out clearly. After a while it fades away.

Then I wonder how to make it bound – how to place within it a splinter of my soul. Hrothgar's book didn't explain how to do that. But I have a moment of inspiration. It must all depend upon the use of imagination again. I must *imagine* myself within it. I must try to look out through its eyes.

Three more times I flicker that spot of moving light into being. But it is no larger and I am wearying. Neither can I peer through its eyes. I become very tired.

That night, before I go to sleep, I visualize the tulpa with my mind's eye. I hold it there as long as I can but then I fall asleep. Perhaps I dream about it but I awake exhausted and almost too tired to clamber from my bed.

Once more I join my hands together in the darkness of the Temple of Dreams.

At last after three days of concentration, I finally manage to materialize the tulpa.

It's crouching on the tabletop staring up at me. It is still relatively small, no larger than my clenched fist. But once unfurled, its wings are twice the length of its body and they look like black leather. There are no feathers and the wings are closer to those of a bat than a bird.

Its body is covered in black fur and it has arms and legs each ending in taloned hands and feet. When it opens its elongated jaw, its tongue is very pink and its teeth are sharp and white. It is indeed a little wolf with wings!

Then the world lurches and I almost fall from my chair. I am in two places at once. I am staring *down* at the tiny tulpa; I am also crouching on the tabletop staring *up* at my large human body.

It only lasts for a moment but I know that I have achieved what I set out to do. A tiny splinter of my soul is within the head of the tulpa and it is bound to me. But how do I control it? Can I be in two places at once and still retain control over both bodies?

Would I also be able to do that whilst retaining my sanity?

Suddenly the tulpa flutters into the air and flies in fast circles close to the ceiling. After a few moments it disappears.

My heart is bursting with elation at my achievement! I wish Hrothgar was here to see what I have done.

18

THE AMBUSH

I wanted to tell Tilda what I had created. I wanted to show off immediately. But then I recognized the sin of pride within me and decided to tell her in the morning.

Despite my tiredness, it took me a long time to fall asleep. The memory fragments of my strenuous efforts to create the tulpa kept circulating in my mind. Again, I saw the tiny but fierce creature materialize on the table. I saw it take to the air and fly in fast circles close to the ceiling.

Then there was that strange moment before it flew when I looked through two pairs of eyes and I knew that I had succeeded in splintering off a piece of my soul.

That was a really strange thing to cope with. But I'd been looking through its eyes so, although I had been worried about a tulpa's similarity to the familiars created by witches, I knew that wasn't the case. The creature was a wraith, something made out of just air using my imagination, and it was a part of me. That was far different to what witches did, feeding a creature and making it subservient to their will.

So I relaxed, feeling pleased with the situation.

No sooner was I asleep than I began to dream.

That dream soon turned into a nightmare.

I was looking through the eyes of the tiny creature again. I was flying high and fast above a wood. It was very dark and there were dense clouds above, blanketing the stars. Despite that, I could see everything below me. Everything glowed with a soft yellow light. My vision was so sharp that I could even count individual leaves.

I was flying very quickly and soon the wood was far behind me and I was over a patchwork of fields. Then I could smell the sea and ahead of me was the long curve of Morecambe Bay, like a giant bite taken out of the County.

I made no decisions – it was as if choices were made elsewhere – but I swooped lower and saw the Caster to Kendal canal below me. I followed it north for a while. Now I knew where I was heading for so I curved away to the left again, flying west, and passed low over the millhouse.

I could see someone walking along the marsh path heading towards Monk's Hill. It was a big man carrying a staff. He was walking with a bad limp. It had to be Spook Johnson and as I flew nearer that was confirmed. As well as limping, he was also walking unsteadily, his shoulders swaying from side to side, and I wondered if he'd drunk too much red wine. In that case, why was he out on the marsh rather than sleeping it off?

As I closed in on Johnson, I saw him stagger and almost fall from the path. It was always slippery underfoot. He could topple at any moment.

At that instant, the dream truly became a nightmare when I saw the water witch.

Hidden by slime, she was waiting in ambush. I could see the shape of her crouching body beneath the soft mud. One taloned hand was already reaching upwards.

I realized that Spook Johnson was too befuddled to notice her, and when she attacked there could only be one outcome. She would surge from the marsh, hands extended, and seize the Spook using the fatal grip that I'd read about in Bill Arkwright's book. The talons would cut upwards through the bottom of the jaw to meet her thumb, which would smash inwards, breaking his teeth. Then she would drag him down into the slime where he wouldn't have time to drown. He would die quickly as she drained him of every last drop of blood.

Her head had emerged from the slime, now revealing her cruel features almost as far as her chin. Her mouth was wide open ready to bite and her yellow fangs looked enormous.

Terrified that I would not be in time to save him, I swooped lower, passing just inches from Johnson's left knee. Then I flew straight at the witch. She was far bigger than I was but I had small hands and small sharp talons of my own. I struck at her eyes but she twisted her head away. I missed, but I did scratch red lines into her forehead, drawing blood.

But I had done enough. Spook Johnson must have seen her jerk away because as I flew clear he blundered towards her, brandishing his big staff, the silver-alloy blade already in position. I saw him stab downwards three times. The first two blows drew screams from the witch. But when he stabbed her for the third time, she was silent – silent, and no doubt dead.

I didn't think Johnson had seen me, although the water witch certainly had. If the creature hadn't flinched away, I would have taken its eyes. Now the Spook stared down at the corpse of the witch. I sped away from the marsh. Faster and faster I flew until everything became a blur. Then I fell into darkness.

I awoke in my bed staring up at the ceiling. The monster under the bed had given me a new habit – now I didn't blow out the candle before climbing into bed. I always let it burn itself out. It wasn't that I was afraid of what might lurk in the darkness, but if there ever was danger it was better to be able to see it.

My fingers felt wet. I held them up before my face and by the flickering candlelight saw that my nails were streaked with fresh blood.

It had been much more than a dream.

The following morning, we'd agreed to go shopping again, but first we went to the Temple of Dreams so that I could show Tilda my progress with the tulpa. As soon as we entered, I told her of that strange experience.

'That could be really useful,' she said, 'to go to sleep and then be able to project your tulpa in such a way.'

'But how did I know that Spook Johnson was in danger?' I asked.

'Well, Wulf, if you can splinter a piece of your soul off like that, it might well be that there are other deeper parts of it that are able to do things you aren't even aware of. Perhaps that's part of your gift?'

'It could be,' I agreed.

'Now! Show me your sky wolf!' she commanded bossily.

I thought it would be more difficult with Tilda watching. Her presence made me nervous and I feared failure. But I needn't have worried. After less than a minute of concentration, and only one count down to zero, the tulpa appeared on the tabletop. Then, once again, it was flying in fast circles very close to the ceiling. But this time I wasn't looking out through its eyes.

It was two or three minutes before it finally disappeared.

'Well done!' Tilda said, giving me a warm smile. 'But there's something that you need to work on – the size of the tulpa. It might be useful to keep it small, but if it could also become larger it could be truly formidable. One day, when we go up against Circe, you might need that . . .'

I smiled and nodded, hiding my true feelings. I knew she desperately wanted to help her parents but there was no way I could imagine the two of us attacking Circe on our own. That was what her mother had tried to do. And look what had happened. Now Alice and Tom were missing, either dead or prisoners in Circe's underworld.

'Look,' Tilda continued, 'why don't I do the shopping by myself and you can stay here and concentrate on developing your skills?'

I didn't like the idea but I could see the determination in her face. I did my best to persuade her against it.

'Make sure you go via the cottage then. And please be careful what you say to the butcher,' I advised her. 'I keep telling you that we mustn't draw attention to ourselves. As we walked away from the shop, a woman came out of the back room and stared towards us. I think it was the butcher's wife or someone who worked for him. Either way, she didn't look best pleased. She might have overheard you. And she would have certainly noticed how cold the shop suddenly was.'

Tilda didn't like being confronted with the truth. I saw the anger in her face. But then I made it even worse by saying something really stupid.

'The sack's really heavy when it's full and it's a steep climb up the hill from the village. It's better if I come with you and carry it back for you . . .'

'I don't need *you* to carry the sack for me! I'm as strong as you are! Why do you always make so much fuss, Wulf? Last time we went down to the village you thought I was going to melt in the rain.'

I had lost the argument and we both knew it.

So Tilda went down to the village alone.

But she didn't come back.

19

THE DARK RIDER

Tilda's trip should have only taken an hour, and so I started to become anxious when she didn't return in time for lunch. Finally, early in the afternoon, with a sinking heart, I left the underworld via the way station and walked down towards the village. It was raining hard, the sky overcast with dark grey clouds.

I halted, hidden high up in a thicket of trees where I had a view of the cobbled main street below with its houses and shops. There were not many people about, which wasn't surprising because of the atrocious weather. But there was no sign of Tilda. I watched in misery, waiting, as water dripped from the leaf canopy and gradually soaked me to the skin. Then, hours later, just as the light began to fail, I had my first glimpse of her.

Tilda was dragged out of the butcher's shop and pushed towards a house further along the street. The butcher and his wife were gripping her by the upper arms. I could see that she was gagged and wore a blindfold. No doubt she had been taken by surprise before she could use her magic. They certainly believed they'd caught a witch and the gag was to stop her casting spells. They shoved her into the house and the door slammed shut.

About half an hour later I saw the butcher mount a horse just outside his shop and then head off in the direction of the northeast. It wasn't too difficult to work out where he was bound for. He was heading for Blackburn to bring the nearer of the two Quisitors back to capture Tilda.

I knew it would take the butcher a couple of hours or more to reach there, and the same back. No doubt the Quisitor, once told about Tilda, would gather his men and arrive here before midday tomorrow. There was no point in waiting longer in the trees so, miserable and desperate, I went back into the underworld, reached my bedroom and tried to sleep.

But sleep wouldn't come. All night I twisted and turned, trying to think what I could do. How could I rescue Tilda from the village? It seemed hopeless, and once in the clutches of the Quisitor it would become impossible.

My best chance was to go now and attempt to rescue her under cover of darkness. Perhaps I could sneak round the back of the house and get in that way? If the door was locked, Saint Quentin would surely get me inside. But there would be others in the house and I'd surely walk straight into their clutches and end up a prisoner myself. Thus my plans remained half-hearted – in truth, frail dreams – and I did nothing. I lay there watching the candle burn low, feeling wretched and cowardly.

At dawn, I drank a little water and left the underworld once more. Soon I was back in the trees looking down at the empty streets of the village. At least the rain had stopped, but the sky was still a dark grey and no doubt some more County rain was on its way.

By now the butcher would have returned. No doubt he was snoring in his warm bed. I wondered about poor Tilda. She would be afraid and probably knew that they had sent for the Quisitor. She would realize exactly what that meant. Tilda would be dragged to Blackburn to face cruel questioning, torture and then burning at the stake.

Noon arrived and still the Quisitor and his men had not arrived. I wondered why they were taking so long. But then, in mid-afternoon, a lone rider entered the village from the north. His hair was shaved on the crown, tonsured like that of a monk, and he was dressed in black. But, unusually, he wore black leather gloves. He also had a long sword at his belt.

Was this the Blackburn Quisitor? It seemed likely.

His horse too was as black as coal and small for its rider. I looked at the horse again and, as he dismounted, I realized my mistake. The horse was *not* small; it was the rider who was big and brawny. The butcher, who I reckoned to be about six feet in height, came out to talk to him. By comparison, this formidable Quisitor had to be nearer seven feet tall.

Surprisingly, he was alone. A Quisitor was usually accompanied by a dozen or so aides. I'd fallen into the hands of Father Ormskirk down in Salford and he'd had an entourage that included both monks and armed mercenaries, not to mention his cruel assistant who was there to torture and execute any witches they captured. So why was this priest alone?

I watched as, still gagged to prevent her casting spells but with her blindfold removed, Tilda was brought out to the Quisitor. Her wrists were already tied together in front of her and the Quisitor fastened a length of rope to that binding and tied the other end to the rear of his saddle. He meant to drag her along behind him. The whole process took just a few moments.

Then he rode out of the village heading northeast towards Blackburn, poor Tilda stumbling along behind his horse.

I circled the village warily until I was following them. I kept my distance, afraid that I would be spotted and the

Quisitor would have two prisoners ready to be tortured in Blackburn. I hadn't a clue how I could rescue Tilda from the clutches of that large armed man, but I couldn't just abandon her. I regretted not eating something for breakfast. It wasn't just that my stomach was rumbling – food was necessary to keep up my strength for this pursuit.

Very late in the afternoon, the narrow path that the Quisitor was following entered the gloom of a wood. Soon I could hear the sound of carrion crows ahead. The birds were on the ground, feeding frantically. As the Quisitor approached, protesting with raucous cries they took to the air and alighted on nearby branches. Suddenly I could see bodies beneath the trees and hear the buzzing of flies. Then I heard a stifled cry from Tilda.

The dark rider halted by each corpse and gazed down on it for a couple of seconds. Was he checking that they were truly dead or had he just returned to gloat at his handiwork? Because by now I had begun to suspect what he was.

When he and Tilda were ahead and out of sight, I paused to examine the dead. There were nine of them, all monks, but there were no marks upon their bodies. They seemed to have dropped dead where they stood. One was just a boy – a noviciate hardly older than I was. Another had a sword in a sheath fastened to his belt and that suggested to me that he was the true Quisitor.

So, what had killed them? The obvious conclusion was that their slayer was the large man on the black horse. After all, he had taken their place. He had caught them on the way to the village and had then ridden on to pose as the Quisitor and take Tilda captive.

Who was he? Suddenly I knew, but I didn't want to believe it. That possibility was too terrifying. But then, after leaving the wood, the rider immediately curved towards the east and then gradually came round until he was riding roughly south. That confirmed my fears. That direction would not bring him back to the Quisitor's base. He was heading more southwesterly and I knew where he was taking Tilda.

He had only pretended to be travelling towards Blackburn. He was really heading for Salford. Beyond that was another underworld – the lair of the evil goddess Circe.

I had feared for Tilda at the hands of a Quisitor but now she was in even greater danger. This was one of the servants of the goddess and, once delivered into her hands, Tilda would die. Circe wanted her special blood – that which she had inherited from her mother Alice, a powerful witch, and her father Tom Ward, who was not just the seventh son of a seventh son but also had lamia blood flowing through his veins.

Circe had many powerful servants. In our previous conflict with her – Tom, Alice and myself – we'd been threatened by the Magi, three large ferocious cat-beasts who were really three kings who had been transformed from their human shape by her magic. This rider that I followed would probably not be human either. What he was I could not guess, but he had slain the Quisitor and his entourage without leaving any external sign of violence, so he was no doubt very powerful.

I dropped further back, keeping my distance, but continued to follow him south. I hadn't a clue how I was going to achieve it, but somehow I had to rescue Tilda before she was taken into the underworld of Circe.

It started to go dark. The rider dismounted and made his camp in a small clearing in the trees. I watched from a distance whilst he unfastened the rope that bound Tilda to his saddle then used it to tie her to a tree. Then he hitched his horse to the same tree and started to collect wood for a fire. He ignited the wood with ease and I suspected he used a similar magic to that employed by Tilda when she lit candles.

Soon he had a fire blazing away and then, after an hour or so when it died down and the embers glowed fiercely, he made a number of high-pitched calls, his voice carrying through the trees. Was he signalling an accomplice?

I soon learned that the calls had another purpose. A rabbit hopped into the clearing and then directly towards him. I watched him slip off his black leather gloves and then, when the small animal was close, he grabbed it and snapped its neck. Soon there were other creatures – another rabbit and a large hare. He killed them quickly and didn't bother to gut or skin them. He didn't use spits for cooking but simply pushed each dead creature into the hot embers.

He didn't wait long before he started eating them either. Their blackened flesh had to be raw inside but he ate greedily, ripping away the fur and tearing flesh from bone ravenously. Tilda had her back against the tree but her head was bowed and she seemed to be looking at the ground. She must be hungry but her thirst had to be far worse. I'd halted for a few moments to drink from a stream but Tilda had drunk nothing and her throat must be parched.

I was weary and lay back in the grass. For what seemed like hours I fought against sleep but, eventually, it overwhelmed me. For a while I knew nothing but blessed relief as my exhausted body slept.

Then, very suddenly, I was alert but I was not in my own body.

I was high above the trees looking down on the clearing where a dark-clad figure was hunched before a fire. I could see Tilda bound to a tree, her head upon her chest.

I was looking through the eyes of the sky wolf which carried a splinter of my soul and was vulnerable to attack. So I descended with extreme caution. Circe's servant might be able to harm me from a distance. After all, those monks had fallen where they stood, the agency of their deaths invisible. If I was slain here, my human body would also die.

I landed on a branch directly opposite Tilda, Circe's black-clad servant stooped over the fire's embers to my left. He was still eating. I was much closer to him now and saw that his hands were not human. Each had three fingers and one thumb. Instead of skin they had green scales, and each digit ended in a sharp yellow talon.

I was partly hidden from him by foliage but had a clear and direct view of Tilda. Suddenly she lifted her head and stared directly towards me and her eyes widened. Then she gave me a brief smile before relaxing, her head resting her chin against her chest, and closing her eyes again.

Tilda knew that I was there but I feared that she might have alerted her captor to my presence. I glanced towards him nervously but saw that he was still feeding. He'd eaten both rabbits and had now started on the hare.

I watched for a while wondering what I could do here in the shape of the sky wolf. Could I free Tilda? That was a possibility. My talons could cut through her bonds. If I could remove her gag she might be able to use her magic against Circe's servant. But could she hope to win in a struggle against him? I didn't know and it wasn't worth taking the risk. My best chance was to wait until he was asleep and then attempt to free Tilda. Perhaps then I could return to my human body and we could both escape before our enemy awoke.

But it was not to be. I was still not skilled enough in practising my gift. Unable to hold my shape, I fell into blackness and the next thing I remember was waking up to see sunlight streaming through the branches above me. In a panic I struggled to my feet. It was at least an hour after dawn and the creature had already ridden away, taking Tilda with him.

Frantically, I began to follow but soon calmed down. I was certain that he was heading for Salford and the underworld of Circe beyond it. Therefore, there was little risk that I would be unable to find him again. I paused and plucked a few mushrooms, the first food I had managed to eat in over a day. Then, soon afterwards, I found edible berries and spent five minutes or so picking and eating those. I also filled my pockets with berries for Tilda – I hoped I'd get the chance to feed them to her.

I had been right to delay my pursuit and eat because soon afterwards I spotted Tilda and her captor in the distance. I followed them although this time I was more cautious and kept further back. I had a long day ahead of me but knew it would be worse for Tilda.

I hoped that Circe's servant would halt and make camp once more before reaching his destination. Of course, he might journey on through the following night and that would mean my last chance to rescue Tilda would be gone. I tried not to think about that.

I need not have feared. The sky was clear and with the sun sitting on the western horizon he finally came to a halt in another clearing and, after binding Tilda to a tree, tethered his horse. He was a creature of habit and followed exactly the same routine as the previous night. After starting a fire, his eldritch calls into the night summoned four rabbits. Their necks were quickly snapped and their furry bodies thrust into the embers.

I watched him eat whilst Tilda was slumped with her back against a tree, her eyes closed. Her thirst must be terrible. Wasn't he concerned about her dying? I thought you could live for about three days without water, but Tilda had been dragged along behind his horse, and even though their progress had been slow, that must have taxed her strength to its limits.

Without waiting for him to finish eating I settled down and tried to sleep, which was easy because I was exhausted after two days of fast walking with very little sustenance. Once more I was looking through the eyes of the sky wolf. I was hovering over the clearing and I could see Circe's servant stretched out asleep close to the embers of the fire, his black gloves removed to reveal his green-scaled hands and talons. Tilda was still in the same position, slumped against the tree.

I landed on the grass facing towards her. I feared to alight anywhere on her body lest she be startled and cry out in alarm, thus alerting her captor. No sooner had I landed than she lifted her head, her eyes opened and she stared towards me. I flew to her left arm and it took just seconds for my talons to cut through the rope that tied her hands together and bound her to the trunk of the tree.

I hovered in front of her whilst Tilda struggled to her feet and tore the gag from her mouth. It took her a great effort and I could see that her whole body was trembling. I glanced anxiously towards the large figure lying by the fire then flew a little way into the trees in the direction I had chosen. Tilda walked slowly after me. I wasn't sure whether her slow pace was due to exhaustion or because she was being careful not to make a noise and thus alert our enemy.

I wanted to get back into my human body but I didn't know how. But the moment that need entered my head I fell into darkness and almost immediately opened my human eyes, scrambling to my feet. I circled the clearing and caught up with Tilda. She was moving slowly so it was easy.

Tilda glanced sideways at me and opened her mouth as if to speak. But nothing but a croak came out. No doubt her mouth was dry and she barely had the energy to breathe. I reached into my breeches pocket and held out a handful of berries towards her. She ate them quickly, desperate for sustenance, but I shook my head when she asked for more.

'Eating too much could make you sick,' I warned her. 'You need water next.'

After a little while we came to a stream and we both knelt and slaked our thirsts there. Then we walked onwards, a little faster than before. Soon the moon came out. It was almost full and lit everything with a silver light.

I wondered if the dark rider was aware of our escape. Tilda's mother, Alice, would have dealt with a pursuit with ease. I remembered how she had conjured up a mist to hide us from the Quisitor's men who'd pursued me. I wondered whether I should tell Tilda that. Perhaps she could do something similar? But one glance at her told me that she barely had the strength to put one foot in front of the other so I held my peace.

Then it was too late. I heard a noise to our rear.

I glanced backwards and saw the dark rider behind us.

'Now I have you both!' he roared out and drew his sword, his horse galloping directly towards us.

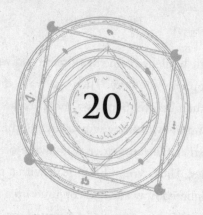

20

THE DARK SHADOW

We both waited there as if rooted to the spot. I was paralysed with fear. Then Tilda raised her arms and tried to chant a spell but her voice was weak and hoarse. It was hardly more than a whisper.

She was going to try to defend us with magic. Could it work against this powerful servant of the goddess Circe?

Tilda achieved something . . .

I watched as a branch swung low like a leaf-claw and struck at the rider's face, but he ducked and pushed it aside with his sword.

Yes, Tilda achieved something but it wasn't enough. He was galloping straight towards her, his sword held aloft as if ready to strike her down. I couldn't let that happen. Suddenly my fear left me and I could move. I ran in front of Tilda, trying to protect her. But I held no weapon. The small blade was still in my pocket, and the rider slashed down towards my head with his sword.

I twisted to one side, attempting to avoid that killing stroke, but I wasn't quick enough. I felt a terrible sharp pain in my head and saw an explosion of light behind my eyes. I felt myself falling and feared that he'd split my skull and cut into my brain. I felt sure that I was dying and sank into a darkness deeper than I had ever known.

Then, once more, I was looking through the eyes of the sky wolf. I was above the clearing and I could see my human body face down where it had fallen. Was I dead? If so, why was I looking through these tulpa eyes? I watched as the dark rider brought his horse round in a tight curve and rode at Tilda again.

She turned to run but he caught up with her easily; his left hand seized her by the hair and pulled her from her feet. She screamed and reached up, trying to force his hand away.

There is a special word to describe the way that a hawk falls out of the sky at speed to seize its prey. The word is *stoop*. A hawk stoops to its prey. It means the hawk folds its wings and drops like a stone at great speed.

Instinctively, that is exactly what I did. I was directly above Circe's servant and fell towards him. As I passed the left side of his head, I opened his cheek with my talons, cutting straight through the flesh to the bone and teeth within.

He swayed in his saddle, cried out and released Tilda who went sprawling to the ground but rolled clear of the horse's hooves. I had already spread my wings and soared aloft, gaining height in order to attack him again.

This time, I came at him directly at head height, flying straight towards his snarling face. My target was his eyes. If I could blind him, then Tilda would be able to escape.

He cut towards me with his sword and I felt the breath of the blade but then I was through his defences, striking at his eyes with my talons. But, like the water witch on the marsh, he twisted away and I missed my target, just scoring blood-filled grooves deep into his forehead. I climbed then. My wings beat frantically, soaring high into the sky above the trees.

I think my intention was to stoop again, like a hawk, and fall upon him at great speed. I wanted to savage his head, his eyes again being my primary target. But I could see him staring up towards me and there was something about him that made me descend more slowly than I had intended.

I glided downwards in slow spirals and then, when I was no more than thirty or so feet above him, I saw my shadow. Cast by the moon, it was gigantic and darkened Circe's creature and his horse. The black shadow of my wings extended some distance to either side of my target. My vision was sharp and I could see the terror upon his face.

I glanced down towards Tilda and saw that she also was staring up towards me with a look of utter astonishment.

In that moment I understood what had happened. The shadow was not an exaggeration caused by the moon and my elevation. I was no longer a small sky wolf. My tulpa had grown into something huge and powerful.

I fell upon my enemy in a fury and dragged him from his horse, which galloped off into the trees, riderless. I heard him scream once – a sound that was quickly silenced as I ripped into him with my talons and teeth. I flew very high before releasing him. I think he must have been dead before he fell, his body seeming to grow smaller, his fingers and feet almost touching, until he was like two small attached sycamore seeds spinning down through the tree branches below.

That done, my eyes grew dark. Had I achieved that in my final moments, my tulpa persisting for a little while as my human body died? I had no regrets. I felt at peace and strangely was not afraid of death.

I had saved Tilda. I was grateful for that.

The next thing I remember was perching on a branch still in my tulpa body. I was gripping the bark with my talons but my eyes were closed. I could hear somebody below me weeping loudly.

I opened my eyes and looked down. I could see Tilda. She was crouching over a prone form on the grass. She was crying without restraint, her body rocking backwards and forwards in anguish. I left the branch and flew forward, hovering so that I could see what her shoulders and head had been obscuring.

What I saw was so shocking that I almost plummeted to the ground. It was my human body and it was dead beyond any possible doubt.

The sword had cut into the skull deeply and the shoulders and neck were covered in blood. I watched as Tilda clambered to her feet still weeping. She walked across and retrieved the sword from the long grass where it had fallen. She then used that to try and dig a grave.

It wasn't easy and took her a long time. I could tell that the grave wasn't really deep enough for the body. It would be easy for some animal to dig it up.

I was in shock, not really taking in what I was seeing. I was looking at my own dead body. I expected to fall into darkness at any moment.

I had been told that once a tulpa realized what it was, the creature would disintegrate and cease to be. But that wasn't so for a bound tulpa, and that's what I now was. A fragment of Wulf's soul still animated me. But how could that continue now that Wulf was dead?

Then I remembered how it had been Hrothgar's servant who had met me and taken me to view his master's grave. Hrothgar's will power had animated the tulpa long after he'd ceased to breathe.

Tilda searched the pockets of my dead body and brought out the feather, the mirror, the notebook and the knife which she pushed into the pocket of her skirt. She dragged my remains into the grave. Then, using her hands, she began to cover the body with soil, the face the last part to be obscured.

Once finished, Tilda came to her feet abruptly and stamped the soil down hard with her boots.

Afterwards, she walked off into the trees. Flying high I followed her. She came to a stream and chose two large heavy stones and carried them back towards the grave. I realized that she intended to use them to protect my grave. I would have liked to help but I lacked hands to carry stones and could only watch the slow process of covering the earth above the spot where my body lay. She never once looked up towards me.

It took Tilda until almost dawn to complete the task. Then she lay down on her side facing the grave and wept again, but eventually her breathing deepened and slowed and she began to sleep.

I felt strangely detached from what had happened. Nothing seemed real and I felt very calm. There was no priest to pray for my departed soul but I took comfort from the way Tilda had behaved. Clearly, she was sad at my passing into the next world and I felt that such grief and concern was as powerful as a prayer uttered by a truly holy bishop.

But I hadn't passed into the next world. I knew that witches went to Hell after they'd died. What about other people who at least tried to be good most of the time? After my dealings with spooks, I didn't believe in God any more, so I had no hope for a Heaven either. Perhaps my soul had passed on, leaving this fragment of me behind?

About three hours after sunrise Tilda awoke. She walked to the stream, knelt and washed her face and hands. After that she went back and knelt again, this time by the side of my grave.

It was then that she looked up and saw me for the first time since I'd killed Circe's servant. Her mouth opened and her eyes widened in astonishment, then she held out her hand, palm upwards. Without hesitation I swooped down and landed on her hand. I was small again and had she made her hand into a fist I would have been enclosed.

'Wulf! Wulf! How is this possible?' she cried, tears falling from her eyes. Then very gently and tenderly she stroked the top of my furry head.

I looked up at Tilda and gave a cry somewhere between a shriek and a croak. But even if I'd been capable of words, I had no answer to her question. And she had called me 'Wulf'. How could I be Wulf when he lay cold and dead in his grave of earth covered by stones?

After a while, despite the lack of communication, we shared an understanding.

I soared aloft and circled Tilda three times. Then we both moved in the same direction. We were heading back towards the underworld that Hrothgar had bequeathed to Wulf.

But I was not Wulf. I was a thing with just a tiny fragment of his soul. Now that he was dead, could we still enter that refuge? We desperately needed to return to safety.

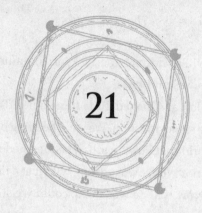

21

HUNTING FOR PREY

We came at last to the two tall sycamores and Tilda walked confidently towards them whilst I flew slowly overhead circling warily.

Again, that moment of doubt came. Would we both be permitted to enter the underworld? After all, I was the one that Hrothgar had bequeathed his house to. So, to make sure, I landed lightly on Tilda's shoulder in case that might help.

I need not have worried. In moments the sky turned the usual baleful red and Tilda was walking through the trees towards the bridge over the moat. I remained on her shoulder as she faced the front door. It yielded to her touch and we entered that refuge.

Tilda made supper whilst I perched on the edge of the table and watched. For her it was shepherd's pie, for me a plate of raw meat. I was hungry and devoured it in less than a minute and it tasted delicious. I realized that I liked the taste of blood. Although I retained his memories, I was no longer Wulf and my needs were far different.

After the meal, without the use of speech, I started to communicate as best I could. I flew to the door of my bedroom and, whilst hovering, scratched at it with my talons. Tilda opened the door and I flew in. When, just moments later, I left that room she closed the door behind me. I scratched again. Now she understood. I wanted the door left permanently open so that I could enter and leave at will. Whether or not my small taloned hands could eventually gain me entry I did not yet know but this made it much easier.

The only door at which I did not scratch that intent was Tilda's bedroom because I respected her privacy.

Then, on returning to the library, I made another demand. I flew high and scratched at the only window in that large room, the one right up in the eaves.

Immediately, Tilda understood. She walked to one of the ladders that were so necessary for retrieving books from the top three shelves, and positioned it directly beneath that window which proved to be stiff. After a struggle she opened it just wide enough for me to fly through.

Moments later I was soaring above the mansion and then I sped towards the twin tall sycamores and entered the human world. I was still hungry and began to hunt for prey.

Although I flew very high, my eyesight was extremely sharp and it didn't take long for me to find food. My kills were small creatures, field mice that were dead before they knew it. But they were exactly what I needed; my sky wolf self found the raw flesh and warm blood delicious.

It was almost dawn before I found anything larger. Rabbits are active at twilight, both before sunrise and after sunset, and it was easy to assuage my hunger. My third kill I did not eat but carried back for Tilda. Shopping in the village would no longer be possible and I would have to provide her with food.

It was only when I reached the window that I realized I had a problem. I was too large to fit through the gap. Whilst I'd been out hunting, my body had adjusted itself to cope with the size of my prey.

It was difficult but I managed to push the dead rabbit through. It fell onto a couple of books, splattering them with droplets of blood, then plunged down to hit the floor. At that moment Tilda came into the library. No doubt she'd heard the noise I'd been making. Quickly, she climbed the ladder and realized the problem immediately. She heaved at the widow until it opened just wide enough for me to squeeze through.

Tilda frowned down at the books immediately below it – the ones stained with blood. She clicked her tongue with annoyance.

'I can see we need to get you housetrained!' she scolded.

Although I knew she was only joking, it angered me as it put me into the category of a pet animal. So I swooped to the floor, fastened my talons into the rabbit and flew it to the kitchen. There I deposited it in the sink.

Moments later, Tilda caught me up and stared at the rabbit. 'Oh! I see! It's for me, is it?' she asked with a smile.

That smile improved my mood and I watched her cook and eat, my own appetite already satisfied. But this time she had to do the washing-up herself. I tried not to feel too pleased about that!

'Right, Wulf,' she said, drying her hands on a towel, 'let's get back to work in the library!'

I followed her there, feeling far from happy. Firstly, I didn't like the way she'd referred to me as *Wulf*. Didn't she realize that I was just a tulpa that might cease to be at any second? Secondly, I had no interest at all in visiting the library. What could I possibly do there that would be of any use?

I perched on the desk feeling miserable whilst Tilda raided the shelves and began to heap books next to me, making pile after pile of reading matter.

'You can perch on my shoulder if you like,' she said, taking her seat at the table. 'You can still read, can't you?'

I looked at the titles of the books on the covers and spines. Yes, I could still read, but I suppose I was sulking and I made no move to do what she'd suggested. I watched as Tilda read, skimming quickly through book after book. She made the occasional note too.

After a while I became bored and flew back to the library then out through the high window. I circled the mansion a few times then left the underworld. This time I flew high over the village, making sure to keep far above the rooftops so that to anyone watching from below I could be taken for a bird.

I hated that place. That was where all our troubles had begun. And I couldn't help feeling that Tilda was partly to blame. She had begun the chain of events that had led to this. If she hadn't spoken to the butcher like that and used her magic against him, then none of this would have happened.

But, gradually, I started to feel better and pushed aside those bitter thoughts. I began to learn new things about flying. I could feel a current of air rising beneath me, its warmth like invisible smoke spiralling from a fire. But then I looked more carefully and saw that the warm air wasn't invisible after all. It was a thermal stream that revealed itself by a subtle shade of brown that clearly differentiated it from the surrounding cooler air.

I looked more carefully at the medium through which I was flying. Below me, I could see strata of air, like thick blankets sliding one over the other, each of a different colour and each at a different temperature that could be used to advantage in flight.

I swooped and tried each in turn, developing my abilities. Flight was a talent that this sky wolf tulpa was born to but it could improve and hone its skills. I spent hours doing so and enjoyed every moment of it. Flying gave me a great sense of freedom, soaring high above the world, feeling the wind on my small body, elevated above creatures forced by gravity to walk, crawl or slither. It was fun and enabled me to forget my problems if just for a little while.

I started to feel sorry for blaming Tilda. I was feeling so much better and was enjoying myself so much that it was a long time before I returned to the library.

Tilda was waiting there. All the books had been returned to their places on the shelves and she was still seated at the table with her arms folded and a look of determination on her face.

'Well, it's just as I suspected,' she told me as I alighted on the table before her. 'You have to ask yourself why you didn't die with your human body and the answer is simple. Your soul was divided between the two bodies, and when the rider killed you with his sword, all of it transferred there!' she said, pointing at me with her forefinger. 'So where does the human end and the tulpa begin?'

I didn't really know what she meant. How could she be sure that I was more than just a splinter of Wulf's soul? There was no way to be sure that my whole soul had transferred, was there? But one thing was clear – even if I was just a tulpa created by my dead human self, I still retained all of Wulf's memories.

'You know what you have to do, don't you?' she demanded, staring at me hard. I couldn't speak but, even if I'd still possessed that capability, I couldn't have answered her question. Because I didn't know the answer.

'Let's see if you've retained your skills. Create a tulpa – you've had plenty of practice so you should find Raphael easy enough to do . . . Go on! What are you waiting for? Use your imagination! Get on with it!'

For a while I did nothing and Tilda just sat there with a patient expression on her face. But after a while I started to concentrate. The process felt no different than when I'd been in my human body. After all, Tilda was right, I'd had a lot of practice manifesting Raphael, who had saved me from the long-armed monster under the bed on my first visit to Hrothgar's underworld.

After a few moments and one slow count from five down to zero, Raphael appeared, hovering above the table, his position maintained by slow steady beats of his huge white wings. Of course, it wasn't the best manifestation of the tulpa I'd ever managed. The blue of his gown wasn't quite as vivid as usual and the metal of the sword did not gleam quite as brightly but it wasn't bad. As he faded away, I felt quite pleased with myself.

Tilda's smile became broader. 'Well done! I knew you could do it! Now all you have to do is create another tulpa – this time a bound one with a human body. It's one you know very well so you should have no difficulty at all in using your memory and your imagination. Create *another* Wulf! Splinter your soul again! Recreate yourself in human form!'

THROUGH THE EYES
OF THE TULPA

I stared at Tilda in astonishment. What she was suggesting was both impossible and crazy. If I'd had the means of speech I would have told her so in no uncertain terms.

Upset and angered by her foolish words, I fled the library immediately and soon, once again, I was soaring above the woods and fields of the human world. I began to hunt once again for prey, the sky wolf dominating the human part of me so that I was more a creature of instinct and emotion than one of rational thought. I hunted rabbits, hares and field mice. In a rush of mindless anger, I killed and killed again, filling myself with warm blood and raw flesh until I was bloated and then, as the sun went down, my body forced me to vomit it all back up.

Afterwards, I perched high upon one of the twin sycamores that marked the entrance to the underworld. I was perfectly still. Only my mind moved, sifting slowly through Tilda's words. After a while I realized that I'd behaved like a sulky petulant child. I felt deeply ashamed.

Then I thought of Tom Ward and how I had been terrified when he had shape-shifted into a lamia and killed the creatures that Circe had sent against us. Because of my fear of that transformation, I had rejected the opportunity to become his apprentice. I now knew that I'd been wrong to do that. He had killed Circe's servants with great ferocity, but in doing that had ended the threat and saved our lives. And what had I done? I had killed those small creatures because of anger and hurt, rather than a need to defend myself or provide myself with food.

I had been wrong about Tom. I had been a coward. I should have become his apprentice.

When I returned to the library Tilda was in her own room, probably lying there awake, angry and disappointed at me. She had meant well. She'd tried to help me find a way out of my misery.

I alighted on the desk and brought all my concentration to bear on the task that she had set. I'd never been one to gaze long into mirrors; as far as my personal appearance went, I'd never committed the sin of vanity. Not that I'd anything to be vain about. Consequently, I knew more of the inner workings of my heart and mind than I did of the external appearance of the boy called Wulf. But I gathered what memories I could and I attempted to manifest the tulpa.

At first the form was lacking in substance and colour and I could see right through it. It possessed a head, two arms and two legs and wore the habit of a noviciate monk over which was a spook's cloak and hood. I concentrated even harder and then it happened . . .

My soul divided again. I was looking through the eyes of the human tulpa, regarding the small sky wolf staring up at me.

It did not last long but I was astonished and simultaneously filled with real hope. To a certain extent, I had just been going through the motions – I hadn't believed it would happen, but I had owed it to Tilda to at least make the effort. Now I knew that I really could get my human body back. That possibility filled me with strong resolve.

I didn't want to show Tilda my new human tulpa too early and maybe disappoint her. So, as the days went by, I kept my distance from her but at night continued to hunt and provide her with food. Each time she thanked me politely but without warmth.

I suspected that she was hurt by my attitude. Only once did she peer through the open door into the library where I was busy dreaming, imagining and concentrating. At that time, my human tulpa was not there. Then she walked on without speaking, her expression unreadable.

So it was late that night when I finally knocked upon Tilda's door.

'Come in!' she called out.

I obeyed and walked towards her. She had been sitting on the edge of the bed and now she came to her feet, smiled and took a step towards me, opening her arms wide to give me a hug. She looked overjoyed, beaming at me with pride. I realized that although she had kept her distance, she had expected this to happen.

But those arms did not enfold me because, despite intense effort to maintain that form, I'd already vanished. She smiled again and stared up towards where I was now watching her from my perch on the higher of the two window ledges.

'That was good, Wulf,' she said, her face very serious. 'But your nose should definitely be a lot longer, your eyes much closer together and you've forgotten that big purple wart on your chin!'

I stared at her until she grinned and I realized she'd been joking.

I now had two selves. But where did my soul live? Was it divided between the two tulpas?

It took another week before I could keep that new tulpa in the world for more than a minute or so. But it was similar to the process I'd used when working to manifest Raphael. Bit by bit, minute by minute, I slowly improved my creation.

I worked hard and finally achieved what I set out to do. I could look out through the eyes of the tulpa, hear what it heard, smell what it smelled, and eat to satisfy an appetite that was always growing.

But something had changed. Now I could not manifest both tulpas simultaneously. When I looked through the eyes of the sky wolf, the Wulf tulpa ceased to be. The opposite was also true.

I discovered another problem too. Tilda gave me back the items that she'd taken from my dead body. I thanked her and put them back into my pockets.

They stayed there only as long as I remained within the Wulf tulpa. But the first time I transferred into the sky wolf they were gone – they had fallen onto the kitchen floor.

I realized that there could be a way to solve that problem. Just as I could create myself clothes and shoes, it could well be that I could recreate such items as part of the tulpa. But that would take time and I doubted that I could copy a magical item such as the red feather. I feared, at first, that without it Circe might haunt my dreams. But so far, she stayed away.

All this was new and strange. This was not really my human body. It was not as it had been before. But at times it was almost possible to believe that nothing had changed and that I was the same. I had the memories of Wulf. I acted as if I were Wulf.

So, what was the difference?

Surely, I was still Wulf?

It was another two weeks before I developed full control over my human tulpa. Once that was established, I suggested that we go and buy some provisions – but not, of course, from the local village.

'Maybe some of the farms will sell us food?' Tilda suggested.

'It's worth the risk,' I said, sitting at the table and facing Tilda as we finished off our portions of rabbit pie, 'but we'll have to walk far afield and not trust the local farmers. Word spreads fast and soon they'll all know about the witch who was taken prisoner but never reached Blackburn. They'll find the bodies of the Quisitor and his men too. I have a feeling that the vicinity of this underworld will be a dangerous place for a long time. The Church will send monks to search the area and even soldiers might get involved.'

'I'm sorry,' Tilda said after a while. 'All this is my fault. I should have kept my mouth shut in the butcher's.'

'What's done is done,' I told her. 'Anyway, we may not need to risk buying from local farms. There's another village not that far from here just south of Billinge. I think it's called Chadwick Green and it's not on the same road as King's Moss. So, I doubt that there's much communication between the two. They might have heard of the deaths of the Quisitor and his servants but there's hardly likely to be anyone there who'll recognize you. It's a chance worth taking . . .'

'It certainly is. I don't want to seem ungrateful, but it'll be good to eat something other than rabbit and hare!'

Soon after dawn the following day, I set off walking with Tilda but after five minutes or so I chose my other form. I fell momentarily into darkness and once more I was flying far above the trees. Then, after a while, I swooped down and alighted on Tilda's shoulder.

'I hope you're going to help me carry the sack when it's full!' she said but, of course, I didn't reply.

Chadwick Green was a large village with a whole row of shops on a busy main street that were thronged with customers. That was good because it made it unlikely that Tilda would attract any undue attention. I perched on a chimney, alert for danger as she made her purchases. Only as she was well clear and safely on the road back did I manifest my human tulpa and walk alongside her, carrying the sack as she'd requested.

That night we dined on chicken, boiled potatoes and sprouts, the dish skilfully prepared with herbs that Tilda had selected. It was something of a celebration and I felt really happy. But by now I knew Tilda well and could read her moods.

There was something on her mind. As she finished her meal and placed her knife and fork on her plate, she told me what it was.

'You killed Circe's servant with ease,' she told me. 'Can you change the size of the sky wolf at will?'

'When I did that, my change in size just happened. But now I've got quite a lot more control and it's getting better by the day,' I replied. 'Eventually, I think I'll be able to modify my size at will.'

'Then we're almost ready. We can attack Circe in her lair and put an end to her. We could do it soon. My parents could be back in Chipenden within days . . .'

She was motivated by her need to free Tom and Alice. For all we knew they were already dead. But it would have been hurtful to point out a probability that, deep down, she was well aware of. But what she was proposing was reckless so, keeping my voice calm, I tried to talk her out of it.

'Even combining our strength, I don't think it will be enough,' I told Tilda gently. 'Circe is a goddess and, in the end, even your mother couldn't defeat her.'

'You're trying to tell me that I'm not as powerful as my mother?' Tilda said indignantly, starting to raise her voice. I could see the anger building within her but I had to tell her the truth and divert her from this madness.

'You might be one day but you're young, Tilda, and your powers are still developing. If your mother had been there when we escaped in the woods but Circe's servant followed us, he would never have found us. Alice can summon a mist and hide within it. I saw her do it. She hid me from the Quisitor's men. I would have been captured, tortured and executed but for that. And I saw you try to knock the rider from his horse . . .'

I hesitated and bit my tongue but the rest of the words forced themselves out anyway.

'That almost worked but *almost* isn't good enough!'

'That's not fair!' Tilda protested. 'I was weak and dehydrated – I'd been dragged behind a horse for almost two days without water. That's why my magic wasn't strong enough!'

She stormed off to bed. It wasn't the first time that heated words had passed between us late at night. I should have kept my thoughts to myself. I'd been wrong to be so blunt when Tilda was upset about her parents. We often quarrelled when we were tired but I was sad at our disagreement. After such a good day it was a shame for it to end in that way.

23

A Gate to Hell

I awoke soon after dawn. When I came down to the kitchen, Tilda was already poaching eggs and grilling tomatoes. She often managed to get up just before I did.

'Butter some bread!' she called out cheerfully. 'And make sure the slices are thick!'

Although we often rowed at night, in the morning we always pretended that it hadn't happened.

Although, perhaps *pretended* is the wrong word. I think we both honestly put the quarrel behind us. For both of us, each day was a new beginning and the stupidities of the previous day cast not even the faintest of shadows.

Soon we were eating a delicious breakfast. Then I started to make a proposal that brought the hint of a smile to Tilda's face. I hadn't thought it through overnight. I hadn't planned or rehearsed what I said although it had been in the back of my mind. The words just tumbled out but they were good words and it seemed a good plan. At least we would be doing something and that would make Tilda feel better.

'It would do no harm,' I said, 'if I went and took a look over Circe's underworld. Just from the outside, I mean. For all we know she could have abandoned it and gone elsewhere. I could see if there's any activity and the information I gather could be useful when we're finally ready to attack her. She won't even know I've been nearby.'

Tilda nodded. 'That could do no harm,' she agreed. Her expression told me that she was really pleased at my initiative. She'd been itching for us to do something. 'It'll be good to see if there are any changes. But don't take any risks. It would be different if I were with you but I want you back here safe and sound. Promise?'

'I promise.'

'When will you go?'

'As soon as I've finished breakfast.'

'In that case, as you're doing something important you can skip the washing-up.'

She didn't need to make the offer twice. Ten minutes later, I'd left the underworld and was flying south towards Salford.

As I approached Salford, I made a small detour to visit Kersal Abbey, where I'd spent almost a year training as a noviciate monk.

My control over the sky wolf tulpa was increasing rapidly. Not only could I make myself larger, the opposite was also true. I wanted to visit the scriptorium where the monks copied books, a place I remembered well, and so I was no larger than a bumble bee when I flew through an open window and alighted on a ledge.

Of course, there was a danger attached to being so small. I could easily be splattered against a wall but first I had to be noticed and, unlike a buzzy bee, I flew silently.

Twelve monks were seated working in silence, rapt in concentration. The only sound was the scratching of their pens on paper or vellum. I recognized none of them and three of them were just young boys, probably new to the abbey. I remembered that it was only to be expected because fourteen years had passed.

They were supervised by a gaunt, grim-faced old monk with folded arms. Then, to my dismay, I suddenly recognized their supervisor. It was Brother Halsall, the monk responsible for noviciates. He'd been a stern master but he had been kind to me when the Quisitor had me imprisoned and tortured. He'd brought a salve for the burn inflicted on my forehead and tried to support me with sympathetic words.

But time had changed him. He was no longer a robust muscular monk who was still in the prime of life. His hair was grey, his complexion sallow and his body looked frail. Saddened and shocked at his appearance, I flew out through the open window and climbed high above the abbey, increasing my size to that of a kestrel hawk.

Time sometimes caused unpleasant changes and it was worse to be brought face to face with them suddenly, rather than seeing the gradual ageing that affects all mortals on a daily basis. Both my parents were dead and lost in the past. My father had died when I was still young and I used to see his ghost haunting the barn. My mother had passed away when I was in the third month of my noviciate and the monks hadn't let me go home for her funeral. Another fourteen years had passed now but that didn't lessen my sadness.

Contemplating the passage of those fourteen years also brought to mind the dilapidated, abandoned house at Chipenden from which so many spooks had served the County. That filled me with sadness also. Some things could not be reversed. I could never go home to visit my own parents. Brother Halsall could never become young again but I would do all in my power to restore Tom Ward and Alice to their Chipenden home. But I would do it when the time was right – not the premature risky attack that Tilda favoured.

I flew high over Salford following the line of its main street. Far below I could see the large house that Spook Johnson had once worked from. The windows were smashed and someone had nailed planks across the front door. Salford was now without a spook but no doubt many were happy at Johnson's absence, despite the increasing power of the dark. He'd specialized in hunting witches but had sometimes erred in his judgement. Not all the women held in his cells had practised witchcraft and, although the locals had feared his temper, many had also disliked and resented him.

No doubt I never would now write the book that would salvage his reputation. I wondered how he was coping at the mill and what would eventually become of him as he too grew older and less firm like Brother Halsall.

My thoughts were far from cheerful and I now felt an increasing sense of foreboding as I approached the village where the entrance to Circe's underworld was concealed. I noticed that many of the surrounding farms were abandoned. Even fourteen years earlier families had been leaving the area. Now it was worse. Circe was a cannibal and her creatures and familiars also fed upon human flesh. That area of predation had expanded in order to feed those ravenous appetites.

Now the enchanted village was directly below me and it was exactly as I remembered it. It contained a single street: just a few houses, a small church with a large door and a grocer's shop. The whole place looked deserted but that was just magical camouflage. Or, that would be the case if the goddess was still here. That was one of the things I had come here to discover.

I reduced my size to that of an insect again and descended into the small copse of trees on the slope that overlooked the main street. From here I had a clear view of the shop, the church and two or three of the houses.

I settled in the branches of the tallest tree and waited patiently. For what, I didn't know. There was a limit to the time that I could remain here. I'd promised Tilda that I would be back before nightfall and didn't want to worry her by failing to keep that promise.

Although from the outside the village looked abandoned, if I went closer to the shop, I would probably be able to enter Circe's underworld as I'd done previously. Then I would be able to find out whether or not the goddess still resided there. But I'd promised Tilda not to do that – another promise that I intended to keep. And there was another important reason for not taking that risk.

Once inside that petrifying place, there was no guarantee that I could ever leave it again. Alice had once given me two magical magpie feathers bound together. By separating them, it invoked a spell called *exeunt* that released me from Circe's underworld. But I no longer had those feathers, and had no way of escaping.

I had an underworld of my own, a refuge bequeathed to me by Hrothgar. But Circe's was more than a refuge. It was a doorway, a bridge between the dark and the human world – a means for her to prey upon humans. The entrance to that shop was really a gateway to Hell.

I was within minutes of taking to the air and beginning my flight back when I heard disturbing sounds behind me. There was weeping and a sudden shrill cry of pain.

I looked back and saw people descending the hill. I counted them quickly. There were seventeen in all. Four were armed guards and thirteen of them were prisoners: three men, two women and eight children of various ages. Two were little more than toddlers and they were being carried by male adults that I assumed were their fathers.

The cry of pain came again and I saw that it had been uttered by the fifth adult, an old man who was struggling to keep up and was being kicked viciously on the backs of his legs by the big burly guard who walked at his heels. No doubt the prisoners were about to be taken into the underworld.

The adults, at least the younger ones, would become servants of Circe. Their brains would be devoured by the small familiars who would then enter their skulls and control their bodies. But the children were far too small for that. They would become food for Circe and her cannibal servants.

I could not allow that to happen.

I didn't even think about what I was about to do. It was an automatic response.

I flew down from the tree, increased my size significantly and unsheathed my talons. The first guard was dead before he knew it. I killed the next two just as efficiently. The last one ran and almost reached the street but he died before he could cross it.

In my human form, killing even when it was necessary in order to save the prisoners would have been a disturbing and difficult thing to do. But my sky wolf self, despite the fact that it still retained my human memories, felt no such compunctions. It hardly thought about what it was doing and was only concerned with the immediate consequences of its actions. Those deaths would save those innocent people from the horror and death that awaited them.

Would Circe know what had been done to her servants? Would she seek immediate revenge?

Wasting no time, I transferred to my human body. The prisoners must have been terrified when they were captured. By now they were in a panic, having seen my sky wolf form, afraid that they were about to die too. They froze where they stood and regarded me with fearful eyes.

'Go north to Salford!' I shouted. 'Get yourselves to the town. You'll be safe there!'

To be accurate they would be *safer*, rather than safe. How long would it be before Circe, driven by her voracious appetite, turned her attentions to that small town? But I did not say that. I wanted them to have hope.

Within moments, despite their terror at what they'd just witnessed and their obvious fear of me, the group climbed the hill and headed north. By now I was in the shape of the sky wolf again, and from a considerable height I followed them for a while, flying in wide slow circles whilst they trudged towards safety. Then, reducing my size once more to that of an insignificant insect, I returned to my position perched on the highest branches of the tallest tree in the copse overlooking the village.

The dead bodies still lay where they had fallen and the village still looked abandoned. After waiting for about half an hour, I decided that even if Circe did send more of her servants to pursue the two families, enough time had elapsed so that they wouldn't catch them before they reached Salford.

It would be dark soon and I would just about be able to fly home before nightfall and spare Tilda from worrying about me. So, once more taking on the size of a kestrel hawk, I flew north.

As I approached Salford, I was relieved to see that the prisoners I'd freed had now almost reached the edge of the town.

To the west, the sun was an orange orb already low over the Irish Sea and I would be lucky to reach home before it set, so I could expect a scolding from Tilda. Once I'd told her what I'd done I felt sure that she'd quickly forgive me.

It was intuition that made me glance backwards, a sense that I was in extreme danger.

That premonition proved correct.

Three large winged figures were pursuing me and drawing nearer with every second.

Circe had sent her servants to slay me.

24

THE SIN OF PRIDE

My first instinct was to fly faster and leave them behind.

Above all they must not be allowed to discover where my underworld was located. Even if they were not powerful enough to enter my domain, once they knew its location then Tilda and I would never be safe. Circe's servants would always be waiting to pounce whenever we emerged.

I glanced backwards for the second time. They were now much closer. They looked very large too, especially because I was very small. I increased my size significantly and unsheathed my talons.

I should have been afraid. Yes, I was nervous. But I was also excited by the prospect of fighting Circe's servants. Inside this tulpa my mental state was far different than it was within my frail human body. I was still Wulf but I was also something else: something wild and dangerous that liked to take risks and welcomed the chance of hunting and combat.

I turned sharply. Within seconds I was flying directly towards them on a collision course, ready to attack. Now, for the first time, I was able to see them clearly. They were reptilian with green-scaled bodies and wings and snake-like heads and long tails. They resembled the dragons that I'd once seen in an illustrated bestiary of fabled monsters, which had been brought to the abbey to be copied by the monks in the scriptorium. One of the noviciates turned out to be a talented artist who produced drawings in vivid colour that were even better than the originals.

I was flying directly towards them and dragons were supposed to breathe fire from their mouths and nostrils. Would they burn me to ashes before I could rend them with my talons? Was Circe capable of giving them such a devastating offensive ability?

Her magic was certainly very powerful. I remembered how she'd created a trio of huge cat-beasts, transforming them from three human kings into savage, fanged killers. I recollected the witch with a face like a concave moon that Circe had also fashioned to serve her. That witch was able to fly upon a broomstick.

But witches couldn't fly – any spook could tell you that – and flight, of course, had only been possible within Circe's underworld where her magic made almost anything happen. The witch could not have flown in the human world, however, thus showing the limitations of the goddess's magic in our earthly realm. It did give me pause for thought.

Despite the reckless nature of my winged tulpa, the more cautious human aspect of me prevailed.

So, before I came within range of their fanged jaws, just in case they could breathe fire, I swerved beneath the trio of dragon-creatures and dived at speed towards the trees below. It was a huge wood and I'd already thought of a way of using it to kill or incapacitate at least one of my enemies. As I levelled out, flying no more than twelve feet above the ground, they pursued me at speed in single file, one after the other.

There was a grassy track through the wood, a passage that curved left. From above I'd already noticed that it gradually narrowed, the trees closing in on either side. While maintaining my speed, I slowly reduced my size to adjust for that change. The three dragon-beasts were not tulpas and wouldn't have that ability. They were larger than I was when I entered the forest. I was relying on the fact that the other two would just follow the leader. They would be concentrating hard on catching me and would not notice until it was too late.

I was right.

There was a crack like a branch snapping, then a shrill scream behind me, followed by a heavy thud. I slowed, alighted on the ground and turned to face my enemies. Just as I'd hoped, the first of my pursuers had hit a tree trunk with its wing and had been brought crashing to earth. The two creatures behind, shrieking in alarm, soared upwards beyond the tree canopy to avoid a similar fate.

The evil winged beast on the ground was hurt badly and lying on its right side, half of its left wing hanging as low as its head, the bone clearly broken. Taking advantage of its plight, I attacked, ripping out its throat as I passed and ensuring my safety.

Then I soared upwards, my wings beating fast, taking advantage of a convenient current of brown thermal air as I rapidly gained height. Soon I was far above the two remaining dragon-creatures. They were giving mournful cries and circling the trees directly above the place where their companion now lay dying, its red blood soaking into the ground.

I stooped like a hawk towards its prey. I chose my target, folded my wings and dropped like a stone. My second kill proved just as easy as the first. I soared upwards once more as, gushing blood, the dying dragon-creature plunged towards the trees far below.

Elated by my two victories, talons extended for the third kill, I flew straight at my final enemy. I felt full of confidence. I expected to prevail.

I was filled with pride in what I had achieved. I thought I was a lord of the sky. I believed that I ruled all that I could see.

What a vain fool I had become. So stupid! So arrogant! So deluded!

As a noviciate monk, I'd been taught all about sin and how it could destroy the soul and deserve the fires of Hell. There were seven major sins – amongst them anger, greed and envy – but the deadliest of all was *pride*. Lucifer had been a bright shining angel but the sin of pride had brought him tumbling down into Hell.

It was the same for me.

I did not fall into Hell but I misjudged the distance to my target, because that target had already moved. I had underestimated the creature's ability and it skilfully avoided my talons.

Mine missed. But my enemy's talons did not.

I twisted away but they raked the length of my left side, piercing the flesh and scoring deep grooves into my rib bones. In agony I convulsed and fell towards the trees. Shrieking in triumph the dragon-creature swooped after me, intending to slay me.

Its talons struck at my throat but I was no longer there. I was back on the ground – back on two legs in a human form, racked with pain, blood dripping into my boots.

I pushed that agony to the back of my mind and, in desperation, concentrated upon what I needed to do in order to survive. Once more I was standing on the grassy track between the trees facing towards the dead body of the first of Circe's dragon-creatures. That made it more difficult for my adversary. It had to fly over that huge body in order to reach me and it had to take great care not to damage its wings on the trees on either side of it.

The dragon avoided both obstacles with great skill and flew at me, skimming the ground. It struck, its talons extended.

But I was no longer there. What I had attempted had worked. It seemed that whichever tulpa I now summoned could share my soul.

My white wings had unfurled, and I was Raphael. I flew above the creature in the perfect position for the killing stroke. Despite the stiffness in my side, I brought down my sharp sword with great force and struck the head almost clean from the beast's body. Blood splattered up my blue robe. My third and final opponent had been vanquished.

I left the Raphael tulpa the moment the deed was done.

The pain returned as, once more in the shape of the sky wolf, I flew home in agony. The death of my mortal body had not affected the body of the sky wolf – had I not created a bound tulpa, my creation would have died with me, but it had a piece of my soul and I lived on. But now that I had only tulpa bodies rather than a human one, an injury done to one tulpa would affect all the other tulpa forms. I now felt this, to my cost.

The sun went down and darkness came whilst a more terrible darkness tried to close my own eyes for ever. My breathing became laboured and my heart fluttered erratically until, at last, feeling close to death, I passed between the two tall sycamores and the red baleful light of my own sky was above me. I had once feared it but now it welcomed me home.

Painfully, I squeezed through the window into the library and fluttered to the floor like a dying leaf, where I became a human-shaped tulpa again. I had just the strength to call out Tilda's name before I lost consciousness.

I remember little of what happened next. I had a terrible fever and lay in bed, the sheets soaked with my sweat. There were sips of bitter herbs and strange lights that hovered above my head. I rambled and a voice replied, mostly hushing me into silence.

It was the voice of Tilda. Her words mostly made no sense to me, but it was her magic that dragged me back from the brink of death. And at last I understood what she was saying. I looked at her and felt glad just to be in her presence, and so grateful that she had saved my life. As I stared my heart melted as I realized how truly beautiful she was. She appeared like a dark-haired angel, with high cheekbones and a beatific smile.

I saw that this must have been what Alice looked like at a similar age. I could understand how Tom had let himself fall in love with a witch.

'You're not fit to be let out alone!' Tilda said, shaking her head.

I had heard Tilda muttering this to herself several times as she had tended to me but, until now, I had always been too confused or weary to reply. This morning there was a significant change in how I felt. But satisfying my hunger first was more important than defending myself with words.

She sat on the edge of my bed and handed me a bowl of steaming chicken soup. Then I held out my hand for the spoon. It was the first time I'd done that.

'Can you manage to feed yourself now?' she asked.

I nodded and accepted the spoon, starting to sip the delicious soup. I had to take care to avoid spilling it because my hands were shaky. I didn't speak until I had finished every last bit.

I owed Tilda my life. Her herbs and magic had saved me but it had taken several weeks.

This was the first morning when I'd felt strong enough to feed myself.

'Thanks. That was really nice soup,' I said when I'd finished, handing her the bowl and spoon. 'But I *am* fit to be let out alone. What happened to me wasn't through stupidity or recklessness. In my place, Tilda, you would have done the same . . .'

I'd already given her garbled versions of what had happened. I'd narrated my account in rambling fragments, often falling asleep after a few moments. Now, I told her exactly what had happened, beginning with my rescue of the prisoners and ending with the fight against Circe's servants. I recounted the full story in great detail.

For a long time, Tilda did not speak. Then she took the empty bowl and spoon away and returned a few moments later with a glass of water which she handed to me. This time Tilda didn't sit on the edge of the bed. She began to pace back and forth by its side, deep in thought.

At last she halted and faced me directly, staring hard into my eyes. 'You kept your promise and stayed outside Circe's lair,' she said, 'and all that you did, I would have done too.' She smiled. 'Yes, you're still fit to be let out alone!'

Then she reached into the pocket of her skirt and pulled out a piece of paper and handed it to me. I accepted it but, even before I began to read it, I recognized the handwriting.

It was another letter from Grimalkin, the dead witch assassin.

25

THE SLAYERS OF GODS

Grimalkin's letter quickly got to the point.

Alice Deane and Tom Ward are still alive and I finally know where they are being held. We must meet at midnight one night before the next full moon and in the usual place.
 Grimalkin

'The next full moon is nine days from now,' Tilda said, taking back the letter. 'I don't know why Grimalkin thinks such a delay is necessary before meeting, but we can use that time to get you as fit as possible.'

'Then let's start now,' I said, pulling back the blankets and swinging my legs into position on the bedroom floor.

With Tilda's help I took the first few tentative steps that began my steady progress towards full fitness. After that, day by day, I grew stronger and soon I was soaring above the house once more in the shape of the sky wolf. I was a little stiff after each flight, but by the night before the full moon I was ready to meet Grimalkin and play my part in what would happen afterwards.

It was the moment I had feared ever since I had first met Tilda. I hadn't believed that we could win and my close brush with death had done nothing to change my mind.

For although we didn't discuss it, both Tilda and I knew what Grimalkin's letter signified. The time had come to attempt the rescue of Tom and Alice.

We were about to confront Circe.

Walking close, our shoulders almost touching, Tilda and I left the menacing red sky of my underworld to be bathed in the silver light of the moon.

In the shadow of a tree, Grimalkin was waiting for us, but she was not alone.

There was another figure standing by her side; it was a slim girl dressed in the same dark garb as the witch assassin. She too wore a skirt that was divided and bound to each thigh to aid movement. There were also straps across her body containing an assortment of blades and a necklace of thumb-bones around her neck. But for the fact that she was smaller – her head level with Grimalkin's shoulder – they could have been twins. Both looked as if they did not belong to our world. They glowed slightly in the darkness and, to my eyes, looked more demon than human.

'This is Thorne,' said Grimalkin.

Thorne didn't speak. She just stared at us and we stared back.

'You've found my parents?' Tilda asked Grimalkin. 'Are they all right? Where are they?'

'As I told you in my letter, they are alive. And I can take you to where they have been imprisoned by the goddess. But it will be extremely perilous to confront Circe,' Grimalkin told us. 'At the moment her power is very much in the ascendancy. Within the dark, there is always a struggle to determine its ruler. For aeons the Fiend was its undisputed leader and after that a new god called Talkus almost came to dominate it. Following his destruction, the struggle for supremacy was renewed and at last the issue has now been resolved. Circe rules the dark and that means she is stronger than ever. There are many of the dark's denizens who may well support her.'

Then, but for the sound of the wind whistling through the trees, there was silence. There was nothing to add to Grimalkin's grim pronouncement. It was even worse than I'd thought.

'Now I wish to discuss the situation with you alone, Tilda. Come with me,' Grimalkin commanded, giving me a glance that I interpreted as being far from friendly.

As they walked away, Grimalkin draped her arm across Tilda's shoulder in an uncharacteristically loving gesture, almost like a mother to her daughter. The witch assassin and Tilda had spent a long time together so I knew that there must now be a strong emotional bond between them.

Together, they moved into the deeper shadows beneath the trees, leaving me alone with the dead girl called Thorne, who continued to stare at me without blinking.

Was I not to be trusted? Or was there even worse news that Grimalkin wished to spare me? I wondered what terrible thing it was that I could not be permitted to hear.

I felt uneasy in the presence of Thorne and finally spoke to break the uncomfortable silence.

'What chance have we got against such a powerful goddess?' I asked. 'How can we hope to succeed against Circe?'

'Circe will not rule the dark for much longer,' Thorne replied. As she spoke, I saw that her teeth were filed to points like Grimalkin's. 'Grimalkin and I are the slayers of gods!' she continued enthusiastically, beaming at me. 'We killed the goddess Hecate, who some considered to be the Queen of the Witches! And now we shall slay Circe!'

Without doubt, the girl was boasting, but she was full of confidence and what she said was utterly convincing. Had they really killed a goddess?

'How did you kill her?' I asked.

'With extreme difficulty,' Thorne replied. 'It was a struggle but we prevailed. Hecate dwelt within the dark at a crossroads. Here she kept her huge iron cauldron which was the source of all her magical power. I stabbed her in the heart and twisted my blade three times as Grimalkin had instructed, but she was slow to die. Then Grimalkin bashed her head against the rim of the cauldron, attempting to break her skull. When that failed, she pushed her under the caustic liquid that bubbled within it. All the flesh fell from her bones and her skeleton floated to the surface. Then we took her thumb-bones!'

Thorne grinned and touched two of the bones that formed a necklace at her throat. Those she touched were yellow and much larger than the others.

'The two biggest bones that I wear here belonged to Hecate,' Thorne continued. 'They're a potent source of power and will help us when we attempt to slay Circe!'

I was impressed by what Thorne and Grimalkin had achieved but also terrified by them. Thorne was obviously delighted at their prowess and accomplishments, but judged by human standards they were monstrous demonic beings as frightening as Circe.

'Thorne!' Grimalkin called and, without another word, the girl walked off to join her in the darkness beyond the trees. Tilda emerged towards me and we went back between the two tall sycamores into my underworld. We proceeded in silence across the bridge, up the steps and into the house, where we walked directly to the library and sat facing each other across the table.

'Cat got your tongue?' Tilda demanded.

'Well, it's certainly got yours!' I replied, trying to keep my voice calm and steady but not really succeeding. 'And do you really blame me for getting angry? Why did Grimalkin tell you things in private? Don't I deserve to know what we face too?'

I was both hurt and annoyed. I felt sure that Tilda was closer to Grimalkin than she was to me. They had secrets that would always be withheld from me.

'Of course you do, Wulf. I don't blame you for getting annoyed,' said Tilda. 'It's irritating when you aren't trusted.'

'Then Grimalkin doesn't trust me?'

'She's concerned and wary, that's all. Oh, she really doesn't think that you'd *intentionally* betray us or act in any way that might cause us problems. But it's what you *are*, you see. You're no longer human, Wulf, and because of that Grimalkin thinks that you'll be particularly vulnerable to Circe's magic. She might be able to control you, even from a distance.'

'But your mother gave me a magical red feather to keep Circe at bay. Now that I use tulpas for my hosts, there must be some way to keep it with me – or perhaps create a tulpa copy of that feather of my own? Perhaps you could use your magic, Tilda? Or maybe there's something in the library that might help?'

'That feather only worked when you were a creature of true flesh and blood that was born from a human mother. We're surprised that Circe hasn't tried to reach you already.'

'So you don't want me to help?'

'We'd *like* you to help but Grimalkin doesn't think it's worth the risk. Supposing we were battling Circe and then she started to control you? Grimalkin spends most of the time in the dark but she's able to see what's happening in our world. She knows what you are – what you're capable of. She saw you defeat Circe's winged servants and can't take the slightest chance that you'll become a tool of the goddess. It's too dangerous to risk your strength being used against us. And then there's something else that you should think about – your own destruction . . .'

'We're all at risk of destruction, Tilda. I'm no different.'

'Oh yes you are! And there are worse things than death. You could end up as Circe's slave. She's done that before many times – the three Magi that my father destroyed. Once proud powerful rulers, they became servile cat-beasts, and then there's something else. The monster under your bed was your bane – one that could have destroyed you. But what if Circe is an even more dangerous bane – the fate that doomed you even before you were born? She damages, captures or slays all that lie in her path. Perhaps being in that path is your doom?'

'That's crazy, Tilda.'

'Is it, Wulf? Some people believe that our path through life is fixed. But maybe we can avoid our fate. Maybe the worst only happens when we take a step in the wrong direction? So, don't take that step, please.'

We didn't speak for a long time. I wasn't sure whether Tilda believed what she was saying. She was just trying to persuade me not to join her in the battle against Circe.

'Why did Grimalkin wait so long before meeting us?' I asked.

'Her magic is more powerful when the moon is full. And there is an hour in that phase of the moon when she is at her strongest. That's when we will strike at Circe.'

'Look!' I said, as my patience snapped. 'You can't stop me following you!' I was aware of the bitterness in my voice, whilst I stared angrily into her eyes.

'No, I can't, Wulf. But would you really want to do that knowing that you might be used against us? Listen to your conscience and stay here. You know it's the right thing to do. Do you promise?'

I lowered my gaze and stared at the surface of the table. 'I promise,' I said at last, my voice hardly louder than a whisper. 'But where are Tom and Alice being held?'

'It's better that I don't tell you that, Wulf. I know you too well – you'd be tempted to go there, wouldn't you?'

I nodded. She was right.

That was the end of the discussion.

After an early breakfast Tilda left the underworld at dawn to journey to the place where she would meet Grimalkin and Thorne. No doubt it would be close to the location where Tom and Alice were being held. And when they tried to rescue them it would bring about a confrontation with Circe.

Whether or not they defeated Circe, I knew that my time living in my underworld with Tilda was over. She was a close friend and I would miss her badly. Our parting was one brief hug. Neither of us spoke. I couldn't read Tilda's expression but I was far from happy. I felt backed into a corner.

After she'd left, I wandered through the house visiting each room in turn. Finally, I ended up in the library where I paced back and forth until I halted before the staff that I'd left leaning against the wall. I wondered if I'd ever be in a position to return it to its owner, Tom Ward. I badly wanted to help to rescue Tom and Alice.

How could Grimalkin be so sure that Circe would be able to control me?

Of course, the sensible thing would have been to do what Tilda said.

I had to listen to my conscience.

And so I did. I listened to it for all of three hours.

Then I followed Tilda north.

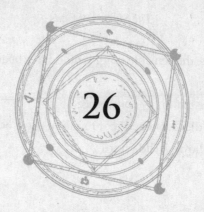

26

THE VERY LAST PLACE

Of course, I didn't know that Tilda was heading north. Not at first anyway. I flew very high in long slow circles until I found her.

She was walking fast and occasionally breaking into a run. I realized that she needed to be at the location for when night fell and the full moon rose into the sky.

I was careful not to underestimate Tilda. After all, she was a witch and would be growing in power the older that she got. What she'd said about being too tired and dehydrated to conjure a spell to stop that dark rider was probably true. A strong and healthy Tilda might well have been able to halt him in his tracks. She had proved her strength by saving me from dying of my injuries.

She might become aware that I was following her, so I kept my distance.

Slowly, I became increasingly puzzled. Tilda was walking towards the very last place that I had expected.

She was now heading directly towards the Spook's house at Chipenden.

On my last visit there, I had found it abandoned and had spent the night in the old bedroom where each Spook's apprentice had slept. It was there that the dead witch assassin had appeared, warning me that I was in danger from Circe and advising me to return to Hrothgar's underworld as soon as possible.

Then, she hadn't known where Tom and Alice were imprisoned by Circe. So why should she arrange to meet Tilda back at that house now?

Tilda reached the withy trees crossroads about an hour before sunset and settled herself down close to the bell. It was still in the position where it had fallen, now almost completely hidden by weeds. Keeping my distance, I watched her nibble at some food whilst she waited. Only when night fell would Grimalkin and Thorne be able to travel here from the dark.

I'd done my very best to keep myself hidden from Tilda, but had Grimalkin been watching me from the dark? If she knew I was here, what would she do?

Gradually the light failed and dusk darkened into night. But then, to my surprise, there was no sign of Grimalkin or her companion, Thorne. The night wore on, the full moon drifting across the sky, hour after hour passing slowly. Had something gone wrong? What could have delayed them?

I could see that Tilda was also agitated because she began to pace up and down beneath the trees. But then I realized she was just impatient for the rescue of her parents to begin and the reason for Grimalkin's delayed arrival suddenly became clear. She was waiting for the precise segment of the full moon when she would be at her strongest.

No sooner had I realized that then, with at best an hour remaining before dawn, I saw two points of light amongst the willow trees. They rapidly grew larger until I saw that they were glowing silver orbs. Did they signal the arrival of a friend or foe?

I had been concerned for nothing, because when they were closer the two silver orbs resolved themselves into the shapes of Grimalkin and Thorne. I realized that it must be the form they adopted to travel here from the dark.

After a short conversation with Tilda, all three of them walked through the trees and entered the garden of the Chipenden house. I gave them a few moments then alighted on the branch directly over the bell. I intended to follow them but was still puzzled as to why they had come here.

I took on my human shape and cautiously entered the garden. Instantly the temperature dropped and I began to shiver. It had been the same the last time I had visited here. I walked on, picking up my pace. There was no warning growl from Kratch, the boggart, but after a while I could hear it whining in the distance.

Grimalkin had told me that it was now blind in both eyes. As far as you could feel sympathy for such a dangerous entity as a boggart, I did feel sorry for it. The creature sounded miserable and in pain. For many years it had guarded the house and dealt savagely with all intruders; now it was blind and seemingly helpless. Did it feel sorrow at failing to protect Tom and Alice?

I crossed the overgrown lawn and walked towards the house, passing the saplings that sprouted up through the unkempt grass. The back door still hung upon its hinges and I stepped inside. It was so cold that it momentarily took my breath away.

I paused to listen, expecting to hear Grimalkin, Thorne and Tilda moving or talking somewhere within. But there was only silence.

I waited a little longer, allowing my eyes to adjust to the gloom, then began to search the rooms, beginning with the ground floor. I did it slowly and carefully, hoping that I wouldn't blunder into the three that I was following – especially Grimalkin. I certainly didn't want to confront her.

I went upstairs and searched the bedrooms one by one. All were empty – not that I wanted to walk in and find anybody there! Finally, I visited the library. That large damp chilly room was particularly sad with its smell of mildew and decaying books. All that lore, all that knowledge of fighting the dark, all gathered by generations of spooks, was slowly rotting away.

There was only one place left to search – assuming that it existed. The big house probably had a cellar. Where else could Grimalkin, Thorne and Tilda have gone? So I needed to find the door that led down to it.

That was far easier said than done. I assumed that access to it would be from the kitchen on the ground floor. I was wrong. What I had previously taken to be the door to a broom cupboard in a corridor opened to reveal narrow stone steps leading downwards. There was a small torch flickering on the wall, evidence that someone had passed this way. So I went down towards a second door at the bottom. I shivered violently. With each descending step, the air grew even colder.

I didn't like the idea of going underground. It reminded me of all the bad things that I'd seen and experienced in Circe's underworld. The confined space meant that I would be severely limited if I took the form of the sky wolf. If doing that, I would need to keep myself small. I wouldn't be able to use the advantage that size gave.

I eased open the door and stepped into the cellar. It was mostly empty – it was clear that the Chipenden spooks hadn't used their cellars to store junk. It contained one flickering wall torch, two small empty crates and an old but serviceable rusty bucket. But the tidy effect was ruined by the huge hole in the far wall with a heap of bricks and earth to the side of it.

It seemed very likely that the final and successful attack upon this house must have come from underground. Someone or something had dug its way into the cellar, breaking through the brick wall that lined it to take the occupants by surprise.

I walked towards the roughly circular entrance, which was about six feet in circumference, to be assailed by a blast of freezing air. What lay within it? Was this another underworld or was this a doorway that led directly to the dark?

The inside of the tunnel was pitch black and so I decided to take the torch from the wall. Tilda had probably ignited it by using her magic. But why hadn't she carried it with her into the tunnel?

Who knew what powers the two dead witches had, and no doubt Tilda could see in the dark or maybe generate light by some other method. But that didn't apply to me. I plucked the torch from its bracket and, holding it high, stepped into the tunnel.

Was I already in the underworld that belonged to Circe? It seemed unlikely as we were a long way from the Salford area. Surely it could not extend so far? But no doubt she was capable of creating more than one underworld.

By the light of the torch, I could see footprints in the soft earth ahead of me, made by Tilda and her two undead companions. But there seemed no end to the tunnel and in the distance was only darkness.

After about a hundred or so paces, I came to a huge oblong door on my left, positioned in the earth of the tunnel wall in a manner that seemed far from natural. There were no joists, no wooden frame, to support it. The door was made of smooth metal rather than wood and so shiny that I could see my reflection in its surface. It had no handle and no lock. It reminded me of the strange door in Hrothgar's mansion but for the fact that its proportions were different, being almost as wide as it was tall.

What was its purpose? It was more like the huge door of a vault in which gold and jewels might be stored for safekeeping. My second guess was that this was a huge prison cell.

Looking at the footprints that had churned the earth directly before it, it was clear that Tilda, Grimalkin and Thorne had paused here to examine it. The footprints continued onwards and I was about to follow them when something drew me towards that huge metal door.

I moved closer and ran my palm across its surface. That was a mistake. It was so cold that I felt intense pain and my hand almost stuck to it. The sensible decision was to move on but some instinct rooted me to the spot. I felt a strong need to see what lay behind that door.

I placed the torch on the ground and concentrated. It took several minutes before my reflection changed. At last that polished surface reflected back an old man in a grey robe with dozens of keys of different sizes hanging from his broad leather belt. I was looking through the saint's eyes.

In the shape of Saint Quentin, I considered the door and its lack of a lock in which to insert a key. I remembered the failure to open Hrothgar's door but, faced with this new challenge, I had a knowledge of locks that failed to shake my confidence. Either visible or invisible, no lock could bar *my* way for ever. There was always a way.

I stretched out my bony hand towards its surface, undaunted by my previous painful experience when touching it.

There was no pain this time although I was still aware of the radiating cold. As I touched the door, I sensed unseen cogs and gears moving within it, well-oiled bars and bolts slowly retracting. Then, under the slightest of pressures from my palm, the huge door swung open silently.

I paused and concentrated once more and, in the shape of Wulf, picked up the torch again. Then I stepped through the open doorway.

I was in a large square room with a very high ceiling. The floor was slippery with ice and it was hard to keep my feet from skidding beneath me. But it was my mind that had to struggle even harder to keep its balance.

My second guess proved to be correct.

The room contained a single prisoner but one whom I had not expected to see.

It was Hrothgar.

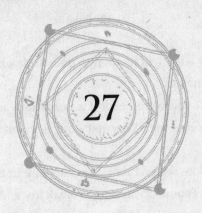

27

SEVEN LONG SILVER NAILS

Hrothgar was alive. Although his eyes were closed, I could see him breathing. The thin giant was standing upright with his back against the tall wall of ice behind him.

He was fastened to the ice by silver chains bound tightly against his body. They were attached to the ice with seven long silver nails, each of which had a broad triangular head made of iron.

There was also a strange symbol inked onto his forehead. It was a five-pointed star with some writing inside. I could understand Latin but this looked like Greek, a language I had no familiarity with at all.

At that moment he opened his eyes and looked at me.

'I'm sorry, Wulf,' he said, his voice shaky and weak. 'All of this is my fault. I'm the reason why you're here now. I'm to blame for what will happen to poor Tilda once Circe has her in her clutches.'

'I thought you were dead!' I accused him angrily. 'Why did you deceive me? Why get your servant to show me your grave?'

'Long before we first met, I was already in the power of the goddess. I could do nothing to break free and was subject to her will. It was she who forced me to send my servant to abduct you. I am not so cruel – I would not have willingly ordered him to break Spook Johnson's leg. Circe commanded that. Her schemes always reach far into the future, predicting and shaping the actions of others so that she will benefit.'

'But you helped me – you saved me from my bane,' I protested. 'But for you I'd have been slain!'

'I had to preserve your life, Wulf. I had to get you past that first threat to your development. That was necessary so that Grimalkin would put Tilda into your keeping in my underworld. It meant that although Circe could not physically enter my domain nor employ her servants there, she knew where Tilda was located and could be ready to snatch her once she left its shelter. I tried to help you in little ways – like returning the red feather – but mostly I worked according to Circe's plan.'

Hrothgar gave a deep weary sigh before continuing. 'But for your intervention, the goddess's servant who seized Tilda would have brought her here weeks ago. That was one thing Circe did not foresee – your rapid maturity as a tulpar and the extent of your abilities. That has astonished me as well. She frequently confides in me so that she can gloat over her triumphs and even sometimes admits her setbacks. When her plan failed, and you rescued Tilda from her captor, in desperation she tore away the magical veil that hides this place so that Grimalkin would eventually find it. She knew that the witch assassin would come here with Tilda to confront her. And that is exactly what has happened. We have all fallen into her trap.'

'My rapid development as a tulpar cost me my life,' I said bitterly.

'Death of the flesh is what happens to all mortals and that also includes those who have our skill to shape bound tulpas,' Hrothgar said. 'But our kind can live on. Until our minds become weary and we no longer wish to live, we can endure a long time upon this earth but not in the bodies we were born into. Not all I told you was a lie. My flesh died long before we first met and of the very disease that I told you about – my heart failed because of my rapid incessant growth.'

Hrothgar sighed. 'I am a tulpa now, in one of the many shapes I can take, but I am vulnerable to Circe's magic. She was unable to enter my domain, but no sooner had you left than Circe summoned me forth and I lacked the power to resist. She forced me to destroy my tulpa servants and brought me here into bondage. She can control me, and now these silver chains and the magical pentacle on my forehead bind me to this spot and lock me into my present shape!'

'Then that's something else you lied about. In one of your books you wrote that you would never create a bound tulpa, that you were afraid to divide your soul!'

'I did not lie. I wrote those words many years ago, before I changed my mind and found the courage to become what I am now.'

I nodded, accepting what Hrothgar said. But my mind was already racing in a new direction. I realized that Grimalkin had been right about my vulnerability to Circe. I'd been wrong to follow them here. I too could be compelled by Circe to become their foe. Then something else filled me with dismay. It was the use of silver and iron to bind Hrothgar's tulpa self. Those metals were also used by spooks to bind creatures of the dark. Was that what I had become?

I reached out my hand towards the nearest of the nails but he flapped his hands and groaned. 'No!' he cried weakly. 'I can only be freed by the will of Circe or by her destruction. Leave me! Go now, and flee this place whilst you still can.'

I dropped my hand back to my side but shook my head. I might not be able to free Hrothgar but I could not leave whilst Tilda was in danger of being captured by Circe. But, because of what I had learned, I was torn between staying and going. If I tried to help, I might be used against them.

'I need to help Tilda. I can't just walk away. Is there any way that I can shield myself against Circe's power?' I asked.

'If there were, don't you think that I would have used it myself?' he asked, his bitter tone showing that he was losing patience with me. 'Leave now before it is too late!'

I nodded. 'Whatever the risks, I can't leave Tilda,' I declared and walked away across the icy floor. Before I reached the door, he called my name.

'Wulf!'

I turned back to face him and saw the pain twisting his face. Up until then he'd hidden that well and distracted me from the truth that he was actually in agony from the contact of the silver. It was painful for him just to speak. But he spoke again anyway.

'There is one possibility that I never got the chance to try, Wulf, because she took me by surprise whilst I was in this shape. It may be useless against her magic but it is better than nothing. For you, there is a difference because you know the threat and can be ready. It may be that if you keep changing your shape when under attack, it could prove more difficult for Circe to overcome you. That's all that I can think of and it offers but a slim hope.'

I thanked him and, leaving the huge door open, departed his prison, turning left to continue along the tunnel. It was still cold but much less so than in the icy cell where Hrothgar was bound. As I walked, I thought over the advice he'd given on how changing shapes rapidly might just enable me to resist the goddess. That could work but, although I could change rapidly between my human and sky wolf shapes, others might be more difficult. I probably lacked the skill to become Raphael fast enough to fend off Circe's power.

About fifty paces brought me to a second door, a much smaller one like the entrance to a farm-hand's cottage. This one was wide open and I followed the footprints inside, which continued on out into the darkness ahead. Grimalkin, Thorne and Tilda had already visited the place beyond that open door.

I knew what was inside. I could smell the metallic odour of blood. I had walked through similar doorways previously when within Circe's underworld.

I held the torch aloft. Atop a big wooden table there was a wooden tray filled with dark red blood and some small pieces of flesh. A small creature had been feeding there. It resembled a spider in shape, but instead of eight legs it had five. The fifth, however, wasn't really a leg – it was a highly specialized appendage which ended in a length of hard bone with a sharp serrated edge. It was a tool used for sawing through a human skull.

The creature had been stabbed several times and was now quite still and dead, lying in a small pool of its own blood.

There was a chair by the table and a broad-chested man, wearing a leather jerkin and hempen trousers, was sitting in it. But the man's body had no head. I could see it where it had rolled into the far corner by the wall, leaving a dark smear of blood across the stone floor.

Until very recently the head would have been attached to the body by a thick piece of gristle and skin. But now the inside of that skull was empty, eaten by the small dead five-limbed creature. I had seen one of these creatures before. It was a familiar called a 'brain guzzler'.

After devouring the brain of its victim, such familiars then lived inside the head. It was a form of possession because the guzzler then controlled the human body. In this case, the guzzler and its host had been servants of Circe. But now were both permanently deceased. Either Grimalkin or Thorne had seen to that. I couldn't imagine Tilda doing such grisly work.

I walked out, glad to leave behind the metallic odour of blood, and followed the footprints. When I came to a third door, I was momentarily annoyed. The footprints showed that Grimalkin, Thorne and Tilda had not even paused in front of it.

My anger cooled. You could not blame them because it was identical to the first door, a huge metal entrance that they had failed to open previously, and they likely thought that attempting to break in was futile. Thus, without wasting time with another fruitless effort, they had ignored it and continued onwards.

But I had two reasons for halting. The first was that I knew that I could open it.

The second was that I guessed who was inside.

It was the prison that confined Tom and Alice.

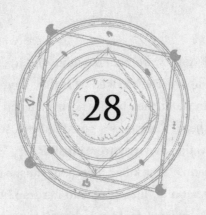

28

A HUGE HAIRY
TALONED HAND

I had no proof that Tom and Alice were locked within it, but
my instincts cried out that I was correct.

Once again, the reflection of Saint Quentin gazed back at
me. I put the palm of my right hand against the cold door
and sensed the cogs turn and the bars and bolts retract. Then
I pushed it open, changed back to my own shape, picked up
the torch again and entered a cavernous room.

Although the cell was very large – much larger than the
one that held Hrothgar – I could only just squeeze inside
because that vast space was mostly filled with ice. My torch
caused thousands of points of red light to be reflected from
its uneven surface but I could still see what was buried
deep inside.

Tom and Alice were bound within the ice, supine and several feet apart. They looked as if they were floating on their backs in water, their bodies horizontal and at about the level of my head. Their eyes seemed to be closed and there was no indication that they were breathing.

So why hadn't Circe killed them? She must have hoped to use their presence to lure Tilda into her trap. And so far it had worked – unless I could somehow intervene.

Again, my instincts were at work and told me that they were not dead but their life was suspended in some way. I wondered whether, like Hrothgar, the destruction of Circe would free them?

Then I saw a glimmer of hope – a manner by which they might eventually be freed without that, although how long it would take was impossible to say. A green shoot, some kind of questing vine, had sprouted from the icy ground at my feet. It had already penetrated several inches into the ice prison and its direction seemed to be towards Alice.

How long had it taken it to penetrate into the ice that far?

I looked closely and could see a fine web of cracks at the point where it entered the wall of ice.

Alice was an earth witch who served Pan, the Old God who ruled Nature. Slow the process might be, but her magic was already working to free her.

But it would not work quickly enough to save Tilda, and so I walked from the ice cavern, turned left again, and continued to follow the three sets of footprints. When the tunnel began to curve to the right I increased my pace, my mind spinning frantically in an ascending and descending spiral of possibilities.

Now that I knew where Alice and Tom were imprisoned, wouldn't it be better to release them immediately? Perhaps the combined magic of Tilda and the dead witches could achieve that? It might just be possible. Also, once free, Alice and Tom would add to our strength. Alice had powerful magic at her disposal and Tom could transform into the fierce lamia shape that had once slain Circe's three Magi servants.

That made good sense. We should free them and then attack Circe. Filled with resolve, I began to walk even more quickly, for a moment sure that was the right thing to do.

I noticed that the tunnel was getting warmer, the heat increasing with every step that I took. And now I was no longer alone but forced to share the space about me with other creatures. Flies buzzed about my head and a moth flew straight into the torch I was carrying, only to be incinerated in a small flare of yellow light.

There were long-tailed rats scurrying in the shadows and a golden lizard stared towards me from the wall on my left, its big bulbous eyes reflecting back the light from my torch.

I remembered this sudden swarming of life from the last time I'd walked along a similar tunnel towards the heart of Circe's underworld. She surrounded herself with all manner of creatures, large and small, some attracted to her presence, others created or changed by her powerful magic. It suggested that she was not very far away.

Soon I heard shouts from ahead and one loud scream. I began to run until a bright circular light came into view. Was it the end of the tunnel? Two figures were in silhouette against that radiance, facing towards it with blades drawn. One was Grimalkin and the other was Thorne.

But where was the third one?

Where was Tilda?

Although bright, the end of the tunnel was opaque and seemed to be filled with a shimmering mist, allowing no view of what lay beyond it. But the nearer I got the more I could see, and there was a dark shadow behind it, something moving that I sensed to be threatening. That was why the dead witches were both holding blades ready to defend themselves.

Then I noticed a large pool of blood on the ground and my heart lurched. Was it Tilda's?

I'd almost reached them when a huge hairy taloned hand thrust its way through the tunnel entrance directly at Grimalkin. She gripped two long-bladed daggers and, with great speed, struck twice, one slicing deep into the palm and the other severing the hairy thumb which fell at her feet. There was a hoarse cry of pain and the hand and arm were quickly withdrawn. I heard something running away, big bare feet slapping the ground.

'Where's Tilda?' I called, and both of them turned to face me.

'She was snatched by Circe's servants out there,' replied Grimalkin, returning her blades to the sheaths on the two leather straps that she wore across her body. 'But we have hurt all three of them badly—'

'Then let's go after her!' I said, stepping towards the shimmering mist.

Grimalkin put a hand on my right shoulder to restrain me. It was very cold and the grip felt like iron so I didn't waste my time trying to shake it off.

'Thorne and I *cannot* go any further. Look! The sun!' she said, pointing towards the light.

She was right. I could see a pale yellow orb through the mist. But that was impossible, surely? 'It was still night when we entered the tunnel. How could the sun have risen so quickly?' I demanded.

'You know yourself that an underworld can change the speed at which time flows. I think Circe has done it to prevent our pursuit.'

Both Grimalkin and Thorne were dead witches and lived in the dark – a place which priests knew by another name:

Hell. By the use of powerful magic, they could visit earth only during the hours of darkness. The light of the sun would destroy them.

'I can still go . . .' I told them.

'Yes, you *could* go, but you would go to your death,' said Thorne, speaking for the first time since we'd entered Circe's realm. 'And if you didn't die, you would become a threat to us. You've already failed to take Grimalkin's advice and followed us. The risk is still there. Circe may be able to wield you as a weapon.'

'But I've got to help Tilda. Look! I needn't fight Circe alone.' I gestured back down the tunnel. 'You passed two large closed doors. I managed to open them. They're still wide open. The nearer one contains Tom and Alice embedded in ice. Could you use your magic to free them? Then in the further cell is my master, Hrothgar. He still lives but is bound with silver chains and a pentacle inked upon his forehead. He has powerful magic and, once freed, might be able to help too . . .'

Grimalkin released me and stared back down the tunnel as if weighing my words carefully. But I was already planning my next move. Yes, I wanted Tom, Alice and Hrothgar freed, but even if that could be done, it would be too late to help Tilda. I needed to free her now before she fell into Circe's hands.

Before Grimalkin could reply, I threw down the torch, dashed through the shimmering mist and was beyond her reach.

The sun, which, when viewed through the mist, had appeared as a pale disc, was instantly transformed. Although very low on the horizon it was still a blazing ball of fire which was far too bright to look at directly.

This was no underworld with a perpetual night and a baleful red sky. I was back in the daylight world but certainly not anywhere within the County. Grimalkin had been wrong. The underworld had not caused time to move forward faster. Circe's powerful magic had made the tunnel emerge in a far different part of the world. The sun was rising and the heat on my face was increasing.

I suspected that this was Greece. After all, the stories and legends about the goddess all claimed that Circe was probably first worshipped in that hot arid land. This was her original home. I looked about me at the dry stony ground, the white rocks and the scattered stunted trees. Then I saw the blood and began to walk, following the red spots shed by the creature that had reached into the tunnel and lost its thumb to Grimalkin's blade.

Circe had many servants but they often worked in groups of three. We had first encountered the three Magi on my last trip here, and later I had fought that trio of winged dragon-beasts. I thought this hairy creature that I was following probably had two companions and that one of them held Tilda captive.

My inclination was to become the sky wolf tulpa. Firstly, I would quickly find and catch up with the creatures that had abducted Tilda. Secondly, no longer being confined by the dimensions of the underground tunnel, I'd be free to increase my size significantly and make the destruction of my enemies possible.

But against this plan was the fact that I knew little about my location and what I faced. Once I took to the air, I would be very visible and other attacks could be directed against me. It was impossible to know whether or not the goddess already knew where I was. But I was not going to make it easier for her, so I continued to follow the spots of blood.

I walked into an area where there were more trees. Their density was not such that I would have called it a wood but they partly obstructed my view ahead. Most of the trees were small compared with those of the County, but their gnarled trunks and branches looked old and no doubt they had been forced to adapt to survive in the arid conditions. And amongst them I occasionally passed much taller thin trees that reminded me of poplars.

There were clouds of flying insects that I had to brush away from my face, and a profusion of beetles underfoot that it was impossible to avoid stepping on. There wasn't the slightest breeze and the heat was gradually increasing too. I longed to take to the skies and feel the cool air beneath my wings, but I resisted and kept to my original decision to follow on foot.

Although uneven, with troughs and hollows, so far the ground had been relatively level but now I began to climb a gradual slope that quite quickly changed into a steep incline. Then the density of the trees increased and restricted my forward vision so that I was no longer able to take the most direct route.

I saw no more spots of blood but it was very unlikely that I was now following precisely in the footsteps of Tilda's abductors. I just hoped we were continuing in the same general direction and that I was catching up with them – that should be the case, as their larger size would make progress through the trees more difficult.

Very suddenly the trees ended and I faced a bare rocky slope with hundreds of stone steps that led to a village perched on the high summit of a hill. The buildings gleamed white in the sunlight, and right at the top was the largest building of all, complete with marble pillars and architecture that pronounced it to be Grecian. It shone like a palace plucked from a tale of princes and princesses, of magic and heroic deeds.

I knew that I'd almost reached the end of my journey, but this was no scene from a wondrous story for the delight and entertainment of children.

Unless they liked nightmares.

I was gazing upon the dwelling of Circe.

Within the walls of her high palace, things spawned in Hell were hiding from the sun.

29

WHITED SEPULCHRES

I began to climb the steep steps. Soon I was breathing hard and sweat was dripping from my brow. At a point about halfway to the top, I was reassured by a trail of blood upon a pale stone. No longer confined to single drops, it assured me that the three wounded servants of Circe had passed this way.

It didn't take long to get proof of that.

Within a few moments I encountered the first of them lying on its hairy back on the steps, as if basking in the sun.

But it was still and dead.

There were severe burns to its massive shoulders and long arms. Its head was little more than a cinder. Had Tilda done that? Was she able to use powerful magic to blast one of her captors? What other explanation could there be – unless someone or something else had intervened? There were cuts to its body too, but they looked like wounds inflicted by Grimalkin's and Thorne's sharp blades.

The steps ended and I began to walk up the steep path of loose stones beyond it. The two-storey houses on either side of me were terraced, each joined directly to its neighbour. But, unlike such dwellings back in the County, they had extremely small windows, most of which were closed with black wooden shutters. The surfaces of their walls were covered with stucco, a white plaster made with lime which, by contrast, made the occasional open door that I passed reveal a room darker than a soul slain by a mortal sin, which was just about as dark as you could ever get.

The Church believed that there were two types of sin – venial sins that spotted the shining whiteness of the sinless soul, and mortal ones that killed it, turning it absolutely black. I shuddered. The insides of those dwellings were mortal-black all right, and I hoped never to be within one.

As I passed by each open door, although I could see nothing within, I could hear disturbing sounds. I could also smell the sharp odour of fresh blood and the faint whiff of rot and decay. Sharp claws scratched upon stone and there was a crunching as if bones were being chewed. I wondered if there were brain guzzlers concealed inside that impenetrable darkness, dining upon the flesh of Circe's victims.

I pondered then how many underworlds Circe possessed. There could be many more than the two that I had visited.

Each would be a predatory tentacle reaching out from the dark into the human world to prey upon humans and feed her familiars and creations. Although I felt the dark would be the hub of all that activity, I wondered again why the underworld from the Spook's house led here, to Greece.

The houses were picturesque on the outside, but similar to the 'whited sepulchres' that the Abbot had often referred to in his tedious Sunday sermons delivered to a crowded chapel full of weary monks. In the County, they were the mausoleums that housed the wealthy dead above ground, ornate and beautiful on the outside but containing rotting flesh and yellowing bones within.

I was just grateful that Tilda wasn't within one of those dark houses – or at least not yet. She would be taken to Circe. Her powerful blood would be reserved for the goddess. Maybe once drained, her flesh and bones would be thrown to Circe's familiars and servants.

Then, as I continued to climb, I reached the second of Tilda's abductors. It was also dead. Its burnt body was face down upon the path with half of its monstrous head blasted away. Again there were deep cuts to its body. No doubt that had weakened the creature, making it easier for Tilda to destroy, but I began to feel hopeful. There was only one left. Perhaps Tilda could deal with that as well?

I began to realize that Grimalkin had been right – one day that girl would be even more powerful than her mother,

Alice. Tilda had been truthful; her failure to deal with the dark rider had been due to her dehydration and general exhaustion.

But for that, things would have turned out very differently. I would still be alive in my human body of flesh and blood. But it was no use dwelling upon such things. What was done was done.

I walked on, wondering again why Circe *was* here in this location with its hot bright sun. It didn't make any sense because the sun would surely harm creatures of the dark – even Circe. After all, she could dwell within the dark and had great power there. As Grimalkin had told me, Circe was now the ruler of the dark itself. She possessed underworlds where her magic and control over their environments was very strong. She had made a witch fly on a broomstick and bound Tom and Alice in a prison of ice.

So why live here? She was unable to venture into the daylight world and I wondered if, like Grimalkin and Thorne, the light from the sun would actually destroy her. If so, she would be confined to her palace. I could think of only one likely reason for her presence here. This must be her first home, the place where she had first become a dark goddess. Perhaps it pleased her to revisit it from time to time?

There was an interesting theory that I had read in one of the relatively few books in Spook Johnson's library that did not have just witches as their subject. According to that tome, it was the act of worship that had elevated such ancient gods and goddesses to the divine. The more that people believed in them, the stronger they became. If that was so, Circe had brought Tilda to the place where her power had begun because she had been believed in. But why had she done that? What purpose would it serve?

The sun was still climbing into a cloudless blue sky. Whilst it shone, I could expect no help from Grimalkin or Thorne. But, if they managed to release Tom, Alice and Hrothgar, those three might be able to come to my aid. It was something that I hoped for but didn't rely upon.

I was on my own for now. Only I would be in time to attempt to save Tilda.

I was approaching the palace at the top of the hill, my feet starting to crunch upon the stones which were piled deeper here. Circe's lair was directly ahead.

The walls of that palace gleamed even whiter than the houses that they towered above and they sparkled as if encrusted with jewels. But the main gate was wide open and it was very unusual. It was round, like a large dark open mouth waiting to devour any who approached it. And a third huge body lay sprawled at its entrance. But one hand, minus a thumb, was very close to that dark doorway. Tilda had clearly killed the third monster, but there was no sign of her. Before it died, it had somehow carried out the will of the goddess, delivering Tilda into her clutches.

Tilda must already be inside the palace.

One glance at that dark doorway filled me with fear. I should have turned and run. I certainly felt like doing that.

Why did my legs keep walking forward?

There were two reasons. I was a young tulpar, inflated with the confidence of my previous successes against Circe's servants. How quickly I'd forgotten what I'd suffered fighting the third of the winged creatures. I also knew that I was too foolish to be deterred.

But neither of those reasons fully explained why I failed to hesitate and do the sensible thing.

I knew that Tilda would be inside.

I swallowed my fear. I did it because of Tilda.

I walked into the dark lair of the goddess.

It took a few seconds for my eyes to adjust to the gloom beyond that open door. There were just four items of furniture in that vast dark hall: a large round table and three chairs positioned round it. Two of those chairs were facing towards me and positioned very close together. They were both occupied, but it was too dark for me to make out who by.

There was a sudden flare of light. Directly above the table was suspended a thirteen-branched candelabra, and each candle was now burning brightly, casting a circle of light down upon it.

In the right chair, Circe was seated, and by her side was Tilda. Already the goddess had worked her devilish magic upon the poor girl. She had no mouth. There was just bare skin from chin to nose. Her eyes were wide open and rolling in her head, revealing her terror at her predicament. This was to prevent her from using spells.

Circe had her right arm about Tilda's shoulders as if to hug her close.

'Approach and be seated!' commanded Circe, her voice echoing from the high walls of the hall. 'It is time to dine!'

My footsteps echoing from the cavernous ceiling, I walked slowly towards the table, noting that it was draped with a cloth of red silk. There was only one dish upon the table and no plates. It was deep and large and empty. Beside it was a long sharp serrated knife and a three-pronged fork such as is used to hold a side of beef when carving. But there was no meat waiting to be carved. There was no dish of gravy.

Tilda and I were the food of the goddess.

I remembered what Alice had once said to me. I'd been telling her about the previous time that I'd sat at a table with Circe and she'd offered me food. It was meat in a thick brown gravy and I hadn't liked the look of it. I had suspected that it was the cooked flesh and blood of Circe's victims. She was a cannibal and so were her servants. Cooking the meat was her concession to me. She liked it raw.

There had been a crypt in that underworld where bones were stored. Some had been stained with blood and a lot of it had been wet and fresh. Alice warned me that if anyone ever sat at Circe's dining table for a second time then they became a victim. Circe had always wanted to drain Tilda's blood because of the power she would gain. I would be another item on the menu.

Circe was staring at me but I did not want to meet her eyes. I sensed her power – and Grimalkin had warned me that because my soul now inhabited only tulpas, I would be very vulnerable to her magic. She would be able to bend me to her will.

So, still carefully avoiding those cruel eyes, my gaze swept over her. She wore a purple dress of fine silk that came below her shoulders and also revealed her bare arms. Her skin was very pale, having never been touched by the light of the sun. I shuddered at what I had noticed previously and had hoped never to witness again. Living things seemed to be moving beneath her skin, like worms slithering within her flesh and weevils, wick with life, scurrying hither and thither. It nauseated me even as my eyes were drawn towards her bright red hair. It confirmed another strange thing that I'd seen before.

It was far from a natural colour. The red radiance was caused by the tiny red mites moving within it, miniscule specs of life ascending and descending each strand of hair. She was a willing host to many entities.

'You have changed, little priest,' she said, her voice a low purr of pleasure. 'You have cast off your weak corruptible flesh and donned something much more suited to my needs. Although above all I require the exquisite blood of the girl who sits beside me, you have something that I desire too! She has the unique bloodline from the father and the mother – that of a formidable witch and also of the seventh son of a seventh son who had the most powerful lamia of all for his mother. But *you* bring something new to my table – something that I welcome. Now be seated!'

Her final words became a loud guttural shout, a harsh compulsive command that I could not counter. My will was snatched away and I did as Circe ordered. I sat in the chair opposite the goddess and Tilda. I was afraid and cowered low in my seat.

'I love creatures about me, all manner of beasts that will do my bidding,' Circe continued, 'and you, priest, have the potential to surpass anything and everything that I have owned before. For you are many wonderful shapes in one. You will be malleable and adapt to my every whim. No longer will I need to use my own magic, slowly shifting the forms of those who serve me – you can do it in an instant.

One command from me and you will instantly accommodate my each and every desire.'

So, I was not to be eaten. My fate would be far different. Tilda had been right. I would be like one of the Magi, the huge cat-beasts who had once been forced to guard her throne and slay her enemies. She would use her magic to hurl me into the sky in the shape of the sky wolf, to carry her messages or hunt her prey. No, she would not eat me. Mine would be an eternity of servitude, obeying each cruel whim of Circe.

'Do you know why I have brought the child here?' Circe said, gripping Tilda by the shoulder.

I shook my head. But I had already thought of just one reason why such a goddess who loved the dark and shunned the light of day should have come to this sun-baked hill somewhere in Greece.

'This is where you began, isn't it?' I asked. 'This is where you first received worship and started to grow in power? So, it pleases you to return here as you become even more powerful.'

'How clever you are, little priest! That is true. But the blood of the daughter of Alice Deane will give me something greater even than enhanced magical strength.'

She opened her mouth and pulled Tilda even closer to her. For a moment I tensed with fear, thinking that she was about to sink her teeth into Tilda's flesh and begin to drain her. But it was just to release the loud triumphant laughter that brayed from her mouth.

'When I have drained this child, I will be able to wander freely in the world – even walk in the sun!' she declared.

I stared at her as I slowly understood the terrible implications of what that meant.

Then she put my thoughts into words.

'When I can walk in daylight, there will be no limits to my power. The whole world of humans will belong to me!'

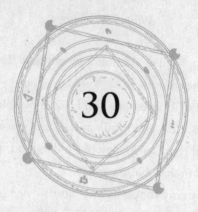

30

THE TRUE NAME OF GOD

Most creatures from the dark were bound within it. Some had a very limited power to briefly visit the earth – but only at night, and usually it was just the exercise of their dark magic at a distance rather than a physical presence. But if Circe were able to walk the earth as she threatened, then the world and all humans would be in thrall to her. If Circe was correct there truly would be no limits to her power.

I spoke without thinking. I asked her a question that even I was surprised by, especially as I'd chosen to leave my noviciate training behind me and had felt sure that I was no longer a believer.

'Aren't you afraid of God?' I asked her. 'If you go too far aren't you afraid that God will intervene and stop you?'

Circe threw back her head and laughed. 'You *would* say that, little priest, wouldn't you? All those foolish monks you lived and prayed with – all those idiots who worshipped an old man with a white beard. I see no sign of him. I have never detected even the merest hint of his presence. He does not exist.'

'God does exist,' I told her. 'But He isn't an old man with a white beard.'

Working at developing tulpas had given me cause to think deeply about the mystery of life and its origins. Now I was starting to put into words what previously had been just vague half-formed thoughts.

She threw her arms wide and smiled at me mockingly. Then she gripped Tilda again, her hand pressing hard into the poor girl's shoulder. I could see spots of blood forming on the material of Tilda's dress where Circe's talons were piercing the skin. 'Perhaps you think that God is female – the mother of all things. That is another foolish idea that some humans favour. Then where *is* your deity, foolish priest? I don't see *her* coming to your aid.'

'God is everywhere,' I told her calmly. 'God is the furnace at the heart of the sun. God is the spark of light radiating from a glowworm on a dark night. I even have a tiny bit of God inside me. It's not much, I must admit, but it's there as surely as I breathe. And I know God's name too. I know the true name of God . . .'

'Do you now?' Circe asked, the mockery strong in her voice. 'Many priests have claimed that over the ages. Many religions have named their deity. Some considered that name too holy to utter aloud. For some it was a closely guarded secret which they took with them to the emptiness and rot of their cold graves. So tell me, little priest. Tell me that name!'

I'd first lost my faith in God as a young child. That loss had riddled me with guilt and shame, spoiling every second of my life so that eventually I'd been forced to confess. But not to a priest. Late one night, when my loud sobbing had brought him to my room, I had confessed that terrible sin to my own father.

He had smiled at my words and placed his arm round me in comfort. 'That's not a sin,' he'd said reassuringly. 'Don't worry yourself, son. *Everybody* doubts the existence of God sometimes.'

I had felt much better after talking to him but, over the years, my faith had continued to wax and wane. And never had it diminished so much as when I became a noviciate monk.

In my long months at the abbey, I had taken part in their rituals, been wearied by the repetitive prayers, bored by the kneeling and standing and sitting and kneeling again. Over and over again they did and said the same things and they repeated them until I became numb and my spirit wilted inside, like a small pot-flower locked in a cellar and deprived of the sun.

No wonder God never answered their prayers. After a day of such worship God would be snoring louder than Spook Johnson!

I remembered the words of the Abbot.

'Imagination belongs to God. It is not for us poor humans to attempt to exercise that faculty.'

When he'd told me that and warned me about writing my own words, that fat lazy pampered Abbot had come very close to the truth. But he hadn't understood the implications of what he'd said. And now, at last, facing Circe, I finally saw it.

I had known it all my life without realizing it. As I answered Circe's mocking question, I reached back deep within myself to grasp the almost untouchable, that small spark within myself. I was also breathing very slowly and mentally counting backwards from five to zero.

I said it very quietly, my voice hardly more than a whisper.

'The true name of God is *Imagination*!'

When I gripped Tilda's hand, Circe was already splattered against the far wall.

Like molten wax, her red flesh and blood flecked with fragments of white bone were slowly sliding down onto the floor behind the table to form a large puddle.

I meant exactly what I'd said. The creation of the universe, the earth, moon and stars, had been a tremendous feat of imagination, the complexity of life drawn forth out of nothingness. What else could God be but that force?

And my true gift was imagination. And what at first I imagined, I could then manifest in the world. My act of creative power had taken Circe by surprise but she was far from defeated and my advantage would not last long.

Still holding tight to her hand, I dragged Tilda towards the open door. Now freed from Circe's grip, the skin covering her mouth had gone. But I still had to get her safely beyond the reach of the goddess.

I sensed a new movement behind me and glanced back to see Circe sprouting from the floor like a monstrous fungus, regaining her shape, red hair rising like snakes. I had done nothing more than delay her for a few seconds.

Then I heard the sound of wood scraping across the tiled floor and ahead of us the huge circular door began to close all by itself. Beyond it was warmth, heat and light – sunlight that was life itself. But I knew I would never reach it.

I pushed Tilda through the narrow gap, sending her sprawling onto the white stones, but I didn't have time to follow her. The door slammed hard, barring my escape, and I turned to face Circe.

I felt both her malevolence and her ill will, the latter threatening to overwhelm me. I was a tulpar but I was no longer in a host of natural flesh and blood. Grimalkin had been right. I was especially vulnerable, and within seconds I could become the mindless servant of the goddess.

This might well be the terrible fate that Tilda had warned me about. Could Circe be my true bane – her threat to me surpassing by far that of the entity I had defeated in Hrothgar's lair? After all, she had entangled me in her schemes right from the beginning. Not only that but, in unwittingly doing her bidding, I had actually contributed to the power she had exerted. And now I could feel her closing in. It was as if I was a little fish alone in an ocean of dark cold water and Circe was casting her net towards me, the fine dark mesh closing in, leaving no room to wriggle free. Within moments she would own me and I would obey her every command.

But I had not forgotten the advice that Hrothgar had offered me – the last slim chance that might allow me to retain control over my own actions.

I changed my form.

The unarmed boy, Wulf, immediately became the formidable Raphael. I was gripping a bright shining sword and, with steady beats of my wings, slowly ascending towards the high ceiling. But, most importantly of all, I had escaped the invisible net. I was free of Circe's attempt to control me.

I was clear of her long sharp talons too, because by now she had fully regained her shape and a swipe of her hand that would have sheared off my left foot barely scraped the bottom of my leather boot.

Then it was *my* turn to attack.

Controlling my wings, I fell towards her at speed whilst bringing down the sharp edge of my sword. Circe tried to twist away but failed and I sliced her head from her shoulders. It fell with a squelch, close to her body, and began to roll away, smearing a thick trail of slimy blood across the tiles.

The goddess fell to her knees. But it was not a result of the blow. It was so that she could reach her head which she quickly returned to her shoulders. As she was rising to her feet, I flew at her again, but this time my wings seemed sluggish and my arms found it difficult to hold the sword aloft. The net was closing in again. Once more Circe was encircling me with the power of her terrible will.

My wings failed me and I plunged towards the ground. Circe attacked, her talons striking towards my face. Just in time, I became the sky wolf tulpa, and my strength returned. No larger than a kestrel hawk, I circled her head and then struck with my talons, slicing open her forehead so that blood ran down into her eyes, blinding her for a few seconds.

I flew higher and increased my size so that I was as large as my enemy. I was big enough to do her serious damage yet not large enough to be hampered by flying enclosed by walls. But as I swooped towards Circe, once again I felt her power. I was heavy and sluggish, an easy target. So I changed back into the form of Raphael.

It was a mistake.

Immediately I learned the limitations of what Hrothgar had advised. I *still* felt weak and slow. Another change back into the boy, Wulf, confirmed my fear. As I desperately backed away, about to be ripped apart by the talons of the gloating goddess, my legs felt too weak to bear me and my will to escape had almost gone.

Yes, a quick change into another host foiled Circe – but it was only a temporary reprieve. I could only use each shape once.

As she lunged at me, I became Quentin. That saint was thin, old and bony, but this time he carried the largest key that he could bear – almost the length and thickness of his grey, hairy arm. It had a sharp point at the end too and I thrust that huge key into the wide-open mouth of Circe, breaking her teeth and stabbing it deep into her throat whilst twisting it as if to unfasten a lock.

The goddess screamed and backed away, but just seconds later my limbs grew heavy and I wanted nothing more than to prostrate myself at her feet and submit to her every whim. I had run out of options, quickly using the limited repertoire of changes that I had developed.

I had nothing left. My struggle was over.

31

THE KILLING GROUND

How I regretted each wasted moment of my time in Hrothgar's hidden underworld. I should have worked harder and tried new forms, developing my skills further. I knew that if I ever survived this, such extensions of my range of shapes were exactly what I would practise.

Desperately, I imagined something very small. I remembered when I'd visited the scriptorium at Kersal Abbey, in the shape of the sky wolf but so minute that I was no larger than a beetle. One glance towards me by any of the monks and that's what they would have taken me for.

One intense moment of concentration, a fast count and a burst of air from my mouth and I was within that new host. I was very small – but my strength was intact. I had become a tiny insect, no bigger than a biting midge that hovers beneath the trees on a warm summer evening. I saw the puzzlement on the face of Circe as for a moment she could not see me. Then her eyes widened as she located her prey. Although too small to do her any harm, I was easily able to escape the hand that tried to enclose me, but the weariness and lack of will were not long in coming. I was soon more than ready to land upon the palm of her hand that she held out towards me.

After that, everything happened very quickly. Time seemed to speed up and, driven by desperation, I reached back into my imagination and pulled things from it that even my deepest nightmares had never shown me. And briefly, sometimes for just seconds, I became them in turn and used those tulpas to try to defeat what could not be defeated. I was as slippery as silk and as sharp as a razor and I fought until I could fight no more. And that moment did not take long to arrive.

I'd come a very long way from my early days of training where I couldn't sustain the life of a tulpa kitten or bring anything into being without long hours of practice and concentration. I'd come a long distance – but not far enough. This was a goddess. This was Circe, the new ruler of Hell. She was too powerful and I could no longer stand against her.

Exhausted by the struggle, I returned to my human shape – once more I was the boy Wulf, dressed in the cloak of a spook's apprentice. I was too weary to change into another tulpa self. I felt slow and vulnerable. I had done my best but now it was over.

I fought her mental net with every remaining fragment of my own will, and at last I turned and ran.

Ran? No. I crawled hopelessly towards the closed door whilst Circe laughed behind me. She was indeed my bane and I was fated to be her servant. Close to despair, I hung on to the hope that Tilda must have survived. If so, what I had done had not been in vain.

I never reached that door. I felt her grasp my hair from behind. And I welcomed it. I had given up. Her will controlled me. I had surrendered. Still gripping my hair, she dragged me to my feet and turned me to face her.

Suddenly the door burst open and crashed back hard against the wall. I didn't see it because I was facing away from it. But my ears left me in no doubt as to what had happened and, despite the pain of Circe's grip, I twisted my head so that I could see it out of the corner of my left eye.

The sunlight had gone. I must have fought the goddess all day without realizing it. Outside it was almost dark, but a pale moon was high over the palace and two silver orbs were floating in through the open doorway.

Orbs that quickly changed their shapes. Two grim glowing demonic figures had entered the hall and Circe was gripped from behind. A powerful arm was across her throat, bending back her head even though she still retained her grip upon my hair. That strong arm, muscles taut and tendons stretched, belonged to Grimalkin, the witch assassin.

Now another smaller figure was at my side. This lithe glowing female was plunging a long blade again and again into Circe's body.

Everything became blurred. Momentarily, I lost my vision and felt myself falling. The landing was not hard and I scrambled up onto my knees quickly, aware that Circe had lost her grip upon me.

We were no longer in the palace of the goddess. Directly ahead was a crossroads crowded by a deciduous forest. This was certainly not the withy trees. I was a long way from Chipenden. At its centre was a huge bubbling black cauldron from which yellow steam rose. It was at least six feet in diameter and shoulder height.

I watched as, together, Thorne and Grimalkin dragged Circe towards the cauldron. She was struggling in their grasp but her movements were weak and blood was gushing from the wounds in her body to splash upon the grass.

Then, suddenly, Circe seemed full of new energy. She broke free and pushed both witches away. They staggered back but as Circe ran at them, talons ready to gouge and tear, Thorne ripped the necklace of bones from her own neck and threw them towards Grimalkin, who caught it deftly and took three long paces to the right. That was enough to cause Circe to choose Grimalkin for her first target.

I knew that the necklace must contain Hecate's thumb-bones, deadly weapons of stored magic that could be used against Circe, who now attacked Grimalkin, bearing her to the ground. But it had been a diversion, a trick, and with an expression of glee, Thorne yanked two big yellow thumb-bones from her pocket and stroked them quickly as she took the power into her own body.

By now, Circe had Grimalkin on her back and was kneeling on her arms whilst choking her by the throat. But having absorbed their power, Thorne cast the bones of Hecate aside and attacked Circe from behind, placing an arm across her throat as Grimalkin had done previously. Now Grimalkin was on her feet and together, once more, they dragged Circe towards the bubbling cauldron.

They tipped her, head first, into the seething liquid, which heaved and hissed and bubbled. For a moment she was totally submerged beneath the surface. Then both of Circe's arms reached out of that caustic liquid. The flesh had gone and nothing but bone remained, but the goddess still managed to grip the rim of the cauldron with both skeletal hands. It was as if, still struggling to survive, she strove to lift herself out.

It was the worst thing she could have done because they were now in a perfect position. Grimalkin drew a short-bladed knife and with two quick strokes severed both of her thumb-bones, which were eagerly grasped by Thorne.

Circe's head burst briefly from the bubbling fluid. Her nose, lips and eyes had gone and so too had her hair. The skin on her face was steaming and bubbling and starting to shrivel. But her tongue emerged from the wide-open bone-cavern of her mouth like a snake and she screamed long and hard until her skull fell back into the boiling liquid.

Grimalkin and Thorne stared at the surface for a long time but the goddess did not emerge again.

It was over. They had destroyed her.

Thorne giggled with delight and, holding Circe's thumb-bones aloft, danced widdershins around the cauldron with childish abandon. And with each step that she took a flower sprouted behind her heels, each a bright yellow primrose. At last she completed the circle and looked up at Grimalkin. They were like a mother and daughter smiling at each other.

'They are yours, Grimalkin!' she cried, holding out the bones towards her. 'Now it's your turn to have the bones of a deity that we've slain! Perhaps now *you* should rule the dark?'

Grimalkin accepted the bones but shook her head. 'I will leave that to another, child. To be a ruler is to be a prisoner of the demands of that office.'

As I scrambled to my feet, Grimalkin turned to look at me. I realized that blood was dripping from my body onto the grass and strips of skin were hanging from my arms. Circe had hurt me and now, for the first time, I felt the agony of my injuries and struggled to hold back cries of pain.

'You still haven't learned to obey, but despite that you did well,' Grimalkin told me. 'The goddess failed to control you and you weakened her whilst we prepared to deal with her. But now we have a problem. We did not intend to bring you here, but Circe still had you in her grip and it was unavoidable. We brought her to this killing ground and you came too. We are now in the dark and it will be difficult to return you to the County.'

I shivered. Until that moment I hadn't realized where I truly was. The dark was what witches called Hell. I was no longer in an underworld located anywhere on earth. This was where damned souls went after death. This was where demons dwelt.

I hadn't walked through a doorway into the dark. Grimalkin's magic had made me fall into Hell.

'We two are dead, and only by the exercise of extreme power can we return to earth and then only during the hours of darkness,' Grimalkin continued. 'Few living people have been returned but Alice Deane was sent back successfully by the Old God Pan and in return she still serves him. But I will try to send you back. If you remain here you could easily fall victim to the dark's denizens, who will regard you as easy prey.'

'We could protect him, Grimalkin!' Thorne cried. 'Give him to me and I will train him in the skills needed to survive here.'

To my relief, Grimalkin shook her head firmly. 'Blood is the currency here and yours, Wulf, is new and fresh and different. They will fight each other to be the first to drink it. Even if we keep you safe from them, few endure for long here and I fear that you may decline rapidly and fall into oblivion. I will try to return you to the cellar beneath the Chipenden house. I hope I can do that and will do my best to align time – but I make no promises.'

The witch assassin raised her arms and I saw sparks at her fingertips. She was exercising her magic to help me. But would it work?

I glanced quickly at each of the four roads that led from the cauldron and into the trees. Each avenue was very long and I could see nothing at the end of them but for a shimmering mist. Suddenly everything began to spin about the cauldron. The crossroads now had eight roads leading from it and, within seconds, far too many to count and just a blur of trees and roads. I became dizzy until very suddenly the movement ceased and once more there were just four exits from where the huge cauldron was positioned at the centre of the crossroads.

Grimalkin pointed down the one to my left. 'Go quickly! Run! Every second will make a difference!'

Aware of Thorne grinning towards me, I nodded and obeyed the witch assassin. Despite the pain from my injuries, I sprinted down the road until I was enclosed by the mist.

As I continued to run, just able to see the ground beneath my feet, I thought of Tilda, Tom, Alice and Hrothgar. Had they been released? Where they safe? I should have asked Grimalkin but it was too late now.

Then there was no ground beneath my boots – just a sensation of falling followed by a sudden jarring jolt.

32

THE SHADOW OF A FROWN

When the mist cleared, I was back in the County, returned to the cellar of the Chipenden spook's house as Grimalkin had promised.

It had changed significantly.

For one thing, the entrance to the tunnel had been sealed. Not only that, every wall had been transformed. Before that they had been lined with old crumbling bricks, but now they'd been replaced with new ones. The work appeared to have been done recently.

I had assumed that the death of Circe had freed Tom and Alice from their ice prison and that they'd been reunited with Tilda. That was my hope.

But surely Tom hadn't had time to block the tunnel and reline the cellar?

Then I looked down at my arms. The pain had gone. There were scars but the lacerations had healed. How much time had passed whilst I'd been with Grimalkin and Thorne?

I walked across the cellar floor and began to climb the steps, emerging from the door onto the corridor on the ground floor of the house. Somewhere above, I could hear somebody hammering and there was a delicious aroma of baking. I sniffed and realized that it wasn't bread. It was a much richer mixture with a hint of spice and something sweet.

When I walked along the corridor and entered the kitchen, Alice was wearing an apron and standing by the table with a big bowl, mixing what was inside with a large wooden spoon. She looked up and smiled at me. I remembered Alice's strained tired appearance when we had last talked in the garden of this house. Now she was fully restored to health and looked hardly older than when I had first met her.

The kitchen was clean and warm and bright with a welcoming fire in the hearth. There were fresh green herbs growing in pots on the window sill. The kitchen looked lived in – a place to cook in and dine in comfort.

'Circe is dead,' I told her. 'Grimalkin and Thorne destroyed her. She's gone for ever.'

'We know,' said Alice. 'We've known for quite a while. The living ain't meant to enter the dark. So Grimalkin found it hard to send you back. The process took time and I've spoken to her twice since then. Of course, for you it might have seemed just a couple of seconds . . . One cake is never enough,' she continued, 'so I'm going to bake another one!'

Suddenly the hammering on the roof became even faster and louder.

'Tom's up there fixing a few tiles. We find a new leak almost every week. They'll all need replacing eventually. All those years of neglect are hard to fix. That takes time too.'

'How much time *has* passed?' I asked her.

'Not too much, Wulf. Ain't nothing to worry you. And Tom and I want to thank you for saving Tilda. We owe you a lot.'

I nodded and smiled but then repeated my question. 'How much time, Alice?'

'It's Tilda's birthday tomorrow,' Alice replied. 'That's why I'm baking the cakes. She'll turn sixteen . . .'

I nodded and smiled. That wasn't too bad. Less than two years had passed. I could cope with that.

'I'd give you a hug, Wulf, but my hands are covered in flour,' Alice said, clapping them together with a smile and creating a white cloud of dust in front of her.

'Then I'll give him a big hug from both of us!' said a voice. I turned towards the door and Tilda came into the room, smiling broadly.

She didn't look that much older than when I'd pushed her through the round door into the sunlight. She was as pretty as ever though, and still walked with her back straight and her head held high as if to defy anybody to be taller than she was. But there was something new in her eyes: a new kind of confidence that was unmistakeable.

She was as good as her word and enfolded me in her arms in the big hug that she'd promised. 'Thank you for saving me,' she whispered into my ear.

But over Tilda's left shoulder the smile had slipped from Alice's face and I could see the shadow of a frown.

I'd fully expected Tilda to stay on indefinitely with Alice and Tom in Chipenden. I was going to miss her but, after all, they were her parents and she'd been separated from them for many years. I'd been surprised when she told me she intended to accompany me when I left.

'You need looking after!' she'd jibed, repeating her old joke. 'You're not fit to be let out alone.'

I'd stayed at the Chipenden spook's house for just over a week. I'd been given my usual room with the green door and the stay had all been very pleasant and restful with great breakfasts cooked by the boggart, despite the loss of both its eyes, and wonderful suppers prepared by Alice and Tilda.

Tom hadn't changed much. He looked young, lean and fit. I'd helped Tom to repair the big house, even fixing some of the tiles myself, and, in return, he'd given me some basic training in fighting with staffs and had directed me to certain books in his library which, despite their long exposure to damp, had now dried out and were mostly readable. It was far more extensive than Spook Johnson's collection and covered the whole range of threats faced by a spook. Reading in there had considerably added to my knowledge of the dark.

But it was the attitude of Alice that had made my stay there feel less than perfect. On the surface she'd been polite and friendly but I sensed a subtle change in the way that she behaved towards me. She'd questioned me closely about what I'd become and seemed satisfied with my answers. But something was bothering her. She didn't say what it was and I lacked the courage to ask her outright.

Then there was another thing that had cast a shadow over everything – it was an increasing threat to Tom Ward. The new witch assassin of the Malkin clan, Makrilda, was Tom's sworn enemy. The first time I'd been on a journey with Tom, Makrilda had followed us for a while but Tom had laughed off the danger.

But now it had become much more serious and dangerous. She'd taken to following him again and now she brought other witches from her clan with her. A few weeks earlier, Makrilda and five others had made an attempt on Tom's life. During his escape he had killed two, but that wouldn't be the end of it. As a spook, Tom often worked alone in the County. Next time there might be even more of them. The job was dangerous enough without that added threat.

I could have tried to do something about it myself or mentioned it to Alice – even though Tom had persuaded me not to do so. But I had another idea . . .

'Where are we going?' Tilda asked as we climbed up into the fells, heading north, a faint drizzle drifting in from the west. The sky was a dark grey and heavier rain was gathering over Morecambe Bay.

I supposed Tilda had thought that we would be travelling to see Hrothgar who had returned to his own underworld to continue his role as a tulpar. And I did eventually want to return here. I wanted more training and my curiosity was piqued by the thought of what could be behind a door that even Saint Quentin had been unable to unlock. But that would have to wait.

'I thought we could pay a visit to Spook Johnson and see how he's getting on,' I said, surprised that she hadn't asked about our destination before.

Tilda nodded but didn't comment. She knew all about Johnson's leg and the difficulties he'd been having adjusting to that.

'I don't think your mother's happy with me!' I suddenly blurted out. As they often did, words had fled my mouth before I'd realized it.

'Why do you say that?' asked Tilda.

'It was hard to put my finger on it but she just seems different, that's all. I don't think she's pleased with me. Have I annoyed her in some way? I wonder if it's because I've changed – because of what I've become?'

Tilda shook her head and grinned at me. 'It's certainly not that. She's just being an anxious mother, that's all. She thinks you and I have spent too much time together and are too close. She came right out and said that to me just before I left. She would rather I'd stayed with her and my father. Mothers can be like that.'

'You should have told me that, Tilda. And you should have stayed at Chipenden, not come with me . . .'

'Don't you want my company?'

'Of course I do.'

'Then don't take my mother's worries to heart. We get on well together, don't we?'

'Of course we do.'

'Then that's all that matters.'

I nodded, but felt uneasy. The next time we called in at Chipenden I would have to speak directly to Alice about it. I wasn't looking forward to that.

On the way to the mill, we left the canal bank for a while and visited a small village called Bolton-le-Sands.

Strangers always attracted curiosity. This time it was the grocer who asked the questions, but Tilda smiled sweetly and deflected his interest politely. Soon we were on our way north again with enough provisions to fill the sack, which I carried over my shoulder.

'Spook Johnson may not exactly welcome us,' Tilda said, glancing at the grey still waters of the canal. It had finally stopped raining. 'He certainly won't be very happy to see me!'

'He got used to your mother and they got on well enough considering that she was clearly a witch. Once he knows that you're her daughter, all will be well,' I said, doing my best to be optimistic. There was a chance that Johnson would prove difficult. The damage to his leg and sixteen years of isolation at the mill were hardly likely to have changed him for the better.

It was late evening when we reached the large post on the towpath; the upper section reminded me of a hangman's scaffold and the huge bell still hung from it, used by locals to summon the aid of Spook Johnson. I wondered how many times he was still called upon.

There we turned left and followed the westerly path beside a fast-flowing stream towards the millhouse. The stagnant moat surrounding it was overgrown with weeds. At one time it had been filled regularly with salt to create a solution that kept water witches at bay. Johnson had never bothered with that. He always did things his own way. Spook Johnson was a law unto himself.

Once we'd waded the shallow moat, we followed a path through thickets to reach the house. Beyond it was the dilapidated wooden mill, the large static wheel rotten and broken. I knocked at the door three times but there was no answer. But the door wasn't locked, so I led the way inside, passing through the storage room to reach the kitchen.

Long before that I heard the snoring. Spook Johnson was certainly at home! He was sitting close to the table, his forehead resting upon it. Beside his head were two empty bottles of red wine. He still had his bulk but there were clear signs that he was ageing. For one thing, there were streaks of grey in his hair.

'Does he wake easily?' asked Tilda.

I shook my head. 'The smell of food is the only thing likely to do that.'

'I'm really hungry, so what do you say if I make my own supper first then, when he wakes up, I'll cook for both of you?'

I nodded and lit the stove for Tilda. Soon she was frying sausages, bacon, mushrooms and tomatoes. When she'd finished, she brought her plate over to the table and started eating. I sat next to her, waiting for the smell of sausages to wake Johnson.

It didn't take more than five minutes. Suddenly Spook Johnson groaned, lifted his head from the table and opened one bleary bloodshot eye. Now the snoring had stopped, all that could be heard was the clatter of Tilda's knife and fork as she ate her supper.

Johnson gazed at me with an expression somewhere between bewilderment and astonishment.

I grinned at him.

'Wulf!' he cried. 'Is it really you? We searched for so long. I never expected to see you again.'

Both his eyes were wide open but now he stared at Tilda.

'What's that girl doing eating *my* sausages?' Spook Johnson exclaimed truculently.

'They're not *your* sausages,' I told him. '*We* bought them and there are plenty more ready to be cooked for your supper when you're hungry . . .'

'I'm hungry now!' exclaimed Johnson.

'Then I'll cook your supper now,' said Tilda mildly, rising to her feet and carrying her empty plate away.

'Do I know that girl?' Johnson asked. 'I feel that I've met her before . . .'

'Tilda looks a lot like her mother, and you did meet her mother, whose name is Alice. Do you remember her?'

'The witch who lives with Spook Ward!'

'Yes, Alice is a witch but she helped us a lot. Do you recall how she rescued you from the clutches of Circe?'

Johnson nodded. 'Yes, I remember it well. When they went missing, I searched for her as well as Tom. I did my best but they were gone for years, and when they came back things were different. I'm not the man I used to be. I don't take kindly to company. Tom Ward came a-calling to tell me they were both safe but he didn't stay long. When he started trying to interfere in my business I lost all patience with him. I didn't want to be bothered so I sent him on his way with a flea in his ear. So I didn't get a full account of what had happened. Is Alice's daughter a witch too?'

'She is, but she's also my close friend, and she could be a friend of yours too if you'll allow it.'

Spook Johnson grunted. I wasn't sure whether he meant yes or no.

Tilda brought in two steaming plates heaped with eggs, sausages, tomatoes and bacon.

Johnson stuck his fork into a big fat pork sausage, brought it close to his mouth and sniffed it warily.

'You'll find it fried to your satisfaction,' I said. 'Tilda is a far better cook than I am.'

'That's not saying much,' he growled before stuffing the whole sausage into his mouth. But within moments he was tucking in and it was a sight to behold. He chewed with gusto, his cheeks bulging with sausage and his forehead beading with sweat. We both ate without speaking whilst Tilda watched us.

At last Spook Johnson finished his meal, belched, pushed away his plate and muttered a thanks to Tilda. Then he fixed his bloodshot eyes on me again. 'Tell me all about it,' he said. 'Tell me what you've been up to and why you don't look a day older than when I last clapped eyes on you.'

I explained what had happened to me in great detail. He didn't comment even when I told him about Hrothgar and how my abduction had been planned by Circe but he raised his eyebrows when I told him about my new abilities and what I had become. Finally, he nodded in approval when I gave him an account of how Tilda, Tom and Alice had been rescued.

Then he just stared at me in silence. I couldn't tell what he was thinking. The silence lengthened. Under the table, to my surprise, Tilda found my hand and gave it a squeeze. I almost jumped from my chair.

It was the first time she'd held my hand like that and I liked it. Her hand was warm; it made me feel really close to her. But my training as a monk made me feel guilty. She was a witch, and holding hands with her couldn't be right. And how would Alice feel about it? Alice's reaction to our friendship was really starting to worry me.

So, to take my mind away from what was happening, I addressed Spook Johnson. 'You don't believe me, do you?' I said at last. 'You're finding it hard to accept that I am what I say I am. Shall I prove it to you?'

The Spook shook his head. 'There's no need for that, boy. I've always found you to be truthful and honest. It's just hard to keep up with so many changes . . .' He came to his feet and started to walk backwards and forwards behind the table, crossing from wall to wall again and again. He had a bad limp and his face was twitching with pain. 'Can't sit in one position for too long. My leg starts to seize up.'

'We came here to see how you were getting on,' I said to him, 'but also for another reason. It's time to go east to sort out the Pendle witches and, with you being an expert on witches, we'd like your help to do it!'

He stopped limping and stared towards me. Years ago, he'd suggested that very same thing and it had been necessary to divert him from that foolish enterprise. There were too many to fight. Taking on the hundreds of witches from the Pendle clans could only end one way. But what I was going to propose was a very limited operation: one that would help Tom and give Spook Johnson a challenge and an incentive to get him back to what he'd once been.

Spook Johnson carried on staring but made no reply. More recently, he had foolishly tried to deal with those witches alone and only survived that encounter when Grimalkin had rescued him. What might that have done to his pride? He considered himself a witch specialist and would find it hard to deal with such a failure – and that on top of his problems with his leg.

To my surprise, he referred to it immediately.

'I tried to deal with them myself, some time ago,' Spook Johnson said, hanging his head. 'It went badly and I was lucky to escape with my life.'

I was surprised that he'd admitted his failure but I noticed that he had not mentioned the part played by Grimalkin.

'Of course, I don't mean we can put an end to all of them,' I continued hastily, 'because there are far too many for that but I think we should deal with the witch assassin of the Malkin clan and her closest supporters. What do you think? Will you help us?'

Spook Johnson straightened his back and a new gleam came into his eyes. He grinned. Then he belched.

'We'll set off at dawn,' he said. 'After young Tilda has cooked breakfast for us.'

I was pleased that he still had fire in his belly but some aspects of him hadn't changed at all. He was still full of self-importance and took other people for granted.

Tilda smiled at him sweetly. He didn't know her well enough to recognize the slight but dangerous tightening of her face in what was suppressed anger. But she had changed like us all. She'd come a long way from the day that she'd insulted the butcher. Her venom was delivered with a subtle smile.

'I'll do the cooking,' Tilda said. 'But you'll wash the dishes!'

JOSEPH DELANEY used to be an English teacher, before becoming the best-selling author of the Spook's series, which has been translated into thirty languages and sold millions of copies. The first book, *The Spook's Apprentice*, was made into a major motion picture starring Jeff Bridges and Julianne Moore.

IF YOU'D LIKE TO LEARN MORE ABOUT JOSEPH AND HIS BOOKS, VISIT:

www.josephdelaneyauthor.com

www.penguin.co.uk

THE SPOOK'S SERIES

WARNING:
NOT TO BE READ AFTER DARK

DO YOU DARE ENTER THE WORLD OF ...

READ JOSEPH DELANEY'S SPOOKY SERIES!

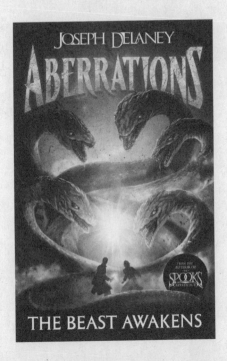

Crafty can't remember a time before the Shole – a terrifying mist that will either kill you or transform you into a terrifying monster, known as an aberration. When Crafty is recruited to join the Castle in the fight against this evil, his life is changed forever . . .